ELON MUSK: A BOOK FOR SMART KIDS

SMART KIDS

Rocketing to the Future: The Visionary Innovator
Shaping Space, Technology, and Beyond

MAGIC MATTHEWS

If something is important enough, you do it even if the odds are not in you favor.

- Elon Musk

Contents

Introduction

Imagine a world where electric cars zoom silently down every road, rockets blast off into space and return to be used again, and humans live on Mars, building a new civilization. These ideas may sound like they come from a science fiction movie, but for Elon Musk, they are part of a real, exciting future. Elon Musk is a visionary innovator who has spent his life working on incredible projects that push the boundaries of technology and imagination. He is constantly asking one big question: "What's next?"

In this book, you'll dive into the life and adventures of Elon Musk, a man who is determined to make the future better for everyone. From his childhood in South Africa to his groundbreaking companies like Tesla, SpaceX, and Neuralink, Elon's story is one of curiosity, hard work, and an unshakable belief that anything is possible. You'll learn how Elon's big dreams led him to become one of the most important figures shaping our world today, whether it's by building electric cars to protect the planet or planning missions to take humans to Mars.

But this isn't just a story about technology. It's a story about never giving up, even when things get tough. Elon's journey shows that even the most successful people face challenges, make mistakes, and experience failure. What sets him apart is his ability to keep moving forward, learning from every setback, and staying focused on the future he believes in.

So, if you're ready to explore the amazing world of Elon Musk — filled with rockets, electric cars, brain-computer technology, and even ideas for living on other planets — then buckle up. You're about to discover the story of a man who's not just dreaming about the future; he's making it happen!

ONE

Early Life: The Young Dreamer

Elon Musk, the man who would one day send rockets into space and build electric cars, was once just a young boy growing up in South Africa. His story starts on June 28, 1971, in Pretoria, a city that is the capital of South Africa. Pretoria might seem far away from the high-tech world of space exploration and electric cars, but for Elon, it was the place where his journey of curiosity, challenges, and big dreams began.

Elon's full name is Elon Reeve Musk, and from the very beginning, his family was full of interesting characters. His mother, Maye Musk, was born in Canada, in a place called Saskatchewan. She was a model and a dietitian, which means she helped people understand what foods were healthy. Maye wasn't just beautiful, though — she was also very smart and always encouraged Elon to be curious about the world around him. Maye's adventurous spirit, especially as a young woman moving from Canada to South Africa, was something that Elon admired.

On the other side of the family was Elon's father, Errol Musk, who was from South Africa. Errol was a man of many talents. He was an engineer who knew how to work with machines, but he was also a pilot and a sailor. He even worked with emeralds, precious green gems, in a business deal at one point in his life. Though there were some stories about Errol owning an emerald mine, many years later, Errol explained that he didn't fully own the mine but had made a deal to receive some emeralds from a small group of mines. Errol's many different jobs exposed Elon to a wide range of ideas, from engineering to flying to working with people in business. He also owned properties, and the family lived a comfortable life when Elon was young.

Elon wasn't the only child in the Musk family. He had a younger brother named Kimbal, who was about a year and a half younger than Elon, and a younger sister named Tosca, who was five years younger than him. The three of them grew up together, and even though they lived in a wealthy family, Elon's childhood was far from easy. Elon also had five half-siblings, meaning children from his father's other marriages, which made the Musk family quite large. After divorcing Elon's mother, Errol Musk married again and had two more children with his second wife. He also became a stepfather to three children from her previous marriage, adding to the number of siblings in the Musk family. This made for a big, blended family with both full and half-siblings.

Elon, Kimbal, and Tosca shared a strong bond growing up, despite the challenges they faced in their family. As the oldest sibling, Elon often took on a leadership role, and while they had different interests, they were united by a shared sense of curiosity and adventure. Kimbal, who would later go on to become a successful entrepreneur in the food industry, and Tosca, who pursued a career in filmmaking, both admired Elon's drive and vision from a young age. Though the Musk siblings went on to lead very different careers, they remain close throughout their lives, supporting one another in their various ventures. However, Elon's relationship with his half-siblings, from his father's later marriages, was less prominent in his life, as he grew more distant from his father over time. While the family was large, it was the connection with Kimbal and Tosca that truly shaped Elon's early years and provided him with companionship and support.

One very special person in Elon's family was his grandfather on his mother's side, Joshua Haldeman, who was an American-born Canadian-South African. Joshua was an adventurer who loved to explore. He even flew his family on exciting journeys across Africa and Australia in a small airplane! Joshua's adventures and curiosity about the world left a strong impression on young Elon. Although Joshua passed away when Elon was only three years old, the stories of his adventurous grandfather sparked Elon's own curiosity about exploration — not just on Earth, but in space too.

Growing up in South Africa in the 1970s was a unique experience for Elon. The country was going through a tough time politically because of apartheid, a system that treated people unfairly based on the color of their skin. Elon's father, Errol, was part of a political group called the Progressive Party, which opposed apartheid. Errol believed that everyone should be treated equally, and he passed these values on to his children. This idea of standing up for what's right influenced Elon later in life when he began thinking about solving big problems for the world.

But life wasn't all fun and adventure for young Elon. Like many kids, he had to go to school, and his school years were tough in more ways than one. When Elon was about eight years old, he started attending a wilderness school in South Africa called "veldskool." The purpose of veldskool was to teach children how to survive in the wild, but it was a very harsh environment. Elon later described it as something similar to *Lord of the Flies*, a famous book about kids stranded on an island who become aggressive and cruel. At veldskool, bullying was common, and children were even encouraged to fight over food. For a young boy like Elon, it was a tough place to grow up, but it also made him stronger.

By the time Elon was nine years old, in 1980, his parents went through a divorce. Divorce can be very hard for any child, and Elon had to decide who he would live with. He chose to stay with his father, Errol. His brother Kimbal also chose to stay with Errol, but Tosca stayed with their mother. For Elon, it seemed like the right decision at the time, but as he grew older, he began to regret it. His relationship with his father became difficult, and they eventually grew apart. Elon would later become estranged from his father, meaning they stopped talking and seeing each other regularly, particularly after he moved to the United States for college and his career. These experiences must have been hard for Elon, but they also shaped him into the resilient and independent person he would become.

Despite living with his father, Elon remained close to his mother. Over the years, their bond grew even stronger, especially as Maye publicly supported Elon's ventures and stood by him during challenging times. Elon frequently credits his mother for her unwavering support and her role in shaping his values of perseverance and independence. Even as Elon pursued his career, Maye continued to be a prominent figure in his life, proudly celebrating his successes and offering her wisdom and love throughout his journey.

When Elon was ten years old, something happened that would change his life forever: he got his first computer, a gift from his father. Computers were very different back then — they were big, slow, and could only do a few things compared to what we're used to today. But for Elon, the computer opened up a world of possibilities. Instead of just playing games, Elon wanted to understand how computers worked. How could they follow instructions? How could you make them do new things? Elon's curiosity led him to teach himself programming. Programming is like giving a computer a set of instructions, called code, that tells it what to do.

Elon didn't just learn the basics of programming — he became very good at it, even though he was only a kid. By the time he was twelve years old, he had created his own video game called *Blastar*. It was a simple game where you had to shoot down enemy spaceships, but for a twelve-year-old, it was an impressive achievement. Elon sold his game to a computer magazine, named *PC and Office Technology*, for about 500 dollars, which was a lot of money for a kid! This moment marked Elon's first step into the world of technology and business, though he probably didn't realize just how far his love for computers would take him.

As Elon grew older, his passion for technology only deepened. While other kids his age were playing outside, he preferred to spend his time on his computer, learning, creating, and dreaming. He wasn't a very social kid, which might have made him feel like an outsider at times, but his interests were helping him build the skills he would need for his future. Elon's imagination was huge, and he wasn't just thinking about games or fun gadgets — he was starting to think about how technology could change the world.

Elon went to several schools growing up, starting with Waterkloof House Preparatory School and then Bryanston High School. Elon changed schools because he struggled to fit in at his early schools and faced bullying from other students. When Elon was about fifteen years old, something terrible happened. One day at school, a group of boys ganged up on him and threw him down a set of concrete stairs. He was badly beaten and had to go to the hospital. It was one of the hardest moments of his childhood, and instead of getting sympathy from his father, Elon later recalled that Errol got angry at him, calling him names and making him feel worse. Errol said that the boy who beat Elon had been going through a tough time and that Elon had called him "stupid," but no matter what happened, the bullying left a deep mark on Elon.

After this incident, Elon was moved to a private school where he could focus more on his studies. He attended Pretoria Boys High School, where he graduated. Even though school wasn't always easy for him, Elon managed to get good grades. He wasn't the top of his class, but he did well enough. For example, he earned a B in math on his senior exams, which is like getting a good grade. However, in Afrikaans, one of the languages spoken in South Africa, he earned a sixty-one, which is more of an average score.

While school may have been challenging in some ways, Elon found comfort in other things — like reading. Elon wasn't like most kids who spent their free time playing outside or watching TV. Instead, he was obsessed with books. He would spend hours reading, diving deep into stories that fueled his imagination. Some of his favorite books were *The Lord of the Rings*, a fantasy epic about heroes and adventures, the *Foundation* series, a sci-fi tale about the future of humanity, and *The Hitchhiker's Guide to the Galaxy*, a humorous and imaginative story about space

travel. These books weren't just entertainment for Elon —
they were windows into other worlds, filled with ideas that
would later inspire his own dreams of space exploration
and technology.

Even though his childhood was filled with challenges —
like bullying, a tough relationship with his father, and the
loneliness of being different — Elon never stopped
dreaming big. His love for books fueled his imagination, his
interest in computers gave him the skills to create, and his
determination helped him push through the hard times.
Looking back, it's clear that these early years, though
difficult, were shaping Elon into the visionary he would
become.

TWO

Moving to North America: Chasing Big Dreams

When Elon Musk was growing up in South Africa, he always dreamed of bigger things. His mind was full of ideas about space, technology, and how to make the world a better place. But South Africa, where Elon was born and raised, wasn't the place where he felt he could make those dreams come true. He knew that if he wanted to chase his big dreams, he needed to go somewhere else — somewhere full of opportunity and innovation. That place, he decided, was North America. Getting there, however, wasn't as simple as just packing his bags and leaving. It would take careful planning, hard work, and determination for Elon to make his way to Canada and eventually to the United States.

Elon's plan to leave South Africa started with an important idea: his mother, Maye Musk, was born in Canada. This meant that Elon could apply for a Canadian passport, making it easier for him to move there and then work his way to the United States. Elon knew that the United States was home to some of the world's best universities and biggest technology companies, so it was the perfect place for someone like him. But before he could even think about going to America, he needed to get to Canada first.

While he was waiting for his Canadian passport application to be processed, Elon didn't waste any time. Instead of just sitting around, he decided to continue his education in South Africa. For five months, he attended the University of Pretoria, a large school in the capital city, where he studied Engineering. This kept him busy while his papers were being sorted out. Finally, in June 1989, when Elon was just seventeen years old, he made the big move to Canada.

Arriving in Canada was both exciting and challenging for Elon. He didn't know many people there, but he had a distant cousin in Saskatchewan, a large province known for its vast farmlands. Elon connected with his cousin and began working various odd jobs to support himself. These jobs were far from glamorous — he worked on a farm and even at a lumber mill, doing tough manual labor to earn money. Life wasn't easy, but Elon was determined. He knew that this was just the first step on his journey to achieving his bigger dreams.

After a year of working these jobs, Elon decided it was time to focus on his education. In 1990, at the age of nineteen, he enrolled at Queen's University in Kingston, Ontario, where he began studying Economics and Physics. This was not a free university, but Elon managed to pay for it by earning scholarships and working part-time jobs. His mother, Maye Musk, also helped by supporting him financially as much as she could. Queen's University was a prestigious school and a great place for Elon to start building the foundation for his future. While studying at Queen's University in Ontario, Canada, Elon met Justine Wilson, a fellow student who would later become his first wife. Justine was a Canadian author with a passion for writing, and the two connected during their time at university. Their relationship grew over time, and they bonded over their shared ambitions and interests. Justine would go on to become an accomplished writer, while Elon's own career was just beginning to take shape. This early connection at Queen's University was an important part of Elon's personal life as he pursued his academic and entrepreneurial dreams.

For two years, he studied hard, learning everything he could and meeting new people. But even though Queen's University was a good school, Elon had his sights set on something even bigger. He wanted to study in the United States, where the technology industry was booming, and opportunities for innovation seemed endless.

In 1992, Elon made the next big move in his life. He transferred to the University of Pennsylvania, a prestigious Ivy League university in Philadelphia. During his time in Canada at Queen's University, Elon focused on his studies and worked diligently, always looking for bigger opportunities. Determined to pursue his dreams, he applied to universities in the U.S., aiming to position himself in a place with greater prospects. His hard work and academic achievements paid off when he earned a scholarship, enabling him to make the jump to the University of Pennsylvania, where he would continue his journey toward innovation and success. This was a major step for Elon, and it opened up even more possibilities for his future. At the University of Pennsylvania, Elon pursued not one but two degrees — he earned a Bachelor of Arts in Physics and a Bachelor of Science in Economics from the Wharton School, one of the top business schools in the world.

Studying Physics allowed Elon to dive deep into the mysteries of the universe, exploring how things work on the most fundamental level. He loved learning about the forces that shape the world, and this knowledge would later help him in his journey to build rockets and push the boundaries of technology. At the same time, his studies in Economics gave him the tools to understand how businesses work and how industries can grow and evolve. This combination of Physics and Economics was perfect for someone like Elon, who wanted to use science and technology to create businesses that could change the world.

Although Elon officially earned these degrees in 1997, at the age of twenty-six, he often mentioned that he completed the work for them by 1995. During his time at the University of Pennsylvania, Elon wasn't just focused on schoolwork. He was also thinking about how he could pay for his tuition and living expenses. Instead of getting a typical job, Elon came up with a creative solution — he started hosting large house parties! He would rent big houses off-campus and throw parties that were so popular, people paid to attend. This helped Elon cover his costs, and it showed just how entrepreneurial he was, even as a student.

But Elon wasn't just interested in parties and schoolwork. He was always thinking about the future, especially how technology could make life better for everyone. During his time at the university, Elon even wrote a business plan for a service that would scan books electronically and make them available online. This was way ahead of its time, as it was similar to what Google would eventually do with its Google Books service many years later. Elon was always thinking about how to use technology to solve problems and create new opportunities.

After graduating from the University of Pennsylvania, Elon faced an important decision. He could continue his education by going to graduate school, or he could jump straight into the world of technology and start building his dreams. In 1994, Elon had a chance to get a taste of what it would be like to work in the tech industry. That summer, he held two internships in Silicon Valley, the heart of the technology world in California. His first internship was at a company called Pinnacle Research Institute, which was working on cutting-edge energy storage technology. They were researching a technology known as ultracapacitors, which are devices that can store energy and then release it very quickly, making them useful for things that need rapid bursts of power. This was fascinating to Elon, as he was always interested in energy and how it could be used more efficiently.

His second internship was at a company called Rocket Science Games, based in Palo Alto. This company wasn't about actual rockets but was working on video games, another area that interested Elon. While at Rocket Science Games, Elon got a glimpse of the fast-paced, creative environment of Silicon Valley, and it sparked his interest in starting his own company one day.

Elon's experiences during these internships gave him a sense of what was possible in the world of technology. He could see that Silicon Valley was a place where people were inventing the future, and he wanted to be a part of it. So, in 1995, Elon applied for a graduate program in materials science at Stanford University, one of the top universities in the world, located in the heart of Silicon Valley. He was accepted into the program, but Elon had something else on his mind — the Internet.

In the mid-1990s, the Internet was still very new, but Elon saw its potential. He believed that the Internet could change the world, and he didn't want to miss out on the opportunity to be part of that change. So, even though he had been accepted into Stanford, Elon made a bold decision: he didn't enroll. Instead, he decided to join the Internet boom, hoping to start his own business in this rapidly growing industry.

Elon's decision to leave Stanford before even starting might have seemed risky, but for him, it was the right choice. He knew that the Internet was going to be a big part of the future, and he wanted to be involved. One of the first things he did was apply for a job at Netscape, a company that was one of the pioneers of web browsers at the time. Elon sent his application but never heard back from them. Instead of getting discouraged, Elon took this as a sign that he should follow his own path.

This decision to skip graduate school and dive into the world of technology would change Elon's life forever. Over the next few years, he would go on to start several successful companies, each one bringing him closer to achieving his dream of changing the world through technology. But it all started with his decision to leave South Africa, move to Canada, and chase big dreams in North America.

THREE

Zip2 and PayPal: The First Big Wins

After Elon Musk made the big move from South Africa to North America, his journey to success really began to take shape. Moving to a new country was a huge step for him, but Elon was determined to follow his dreams. With each step, he moved closer to becoming the visionary entrepreneur we know today. His early days in North

America were filled with hard work, creativity, and some important lessons about business and technology.

In 1995, when Elon was just twenty-four years old, he and his brother Kimbal decided to start their own company. They teamed up with Greg Kouri, a friend, and together they founded a company called Global Link Information Network. This name didn't last for long, though. Soon after, they renamed the company to Zip2, a name that would become much more familiar. At the time, the Internet was still new to many people, and there were a lot of exciting possibilities for creating new online businesses.

Zip2 was a pretty cool idea. Elon and his team wanted to create an online city guide that would help people find businesses, get directions, and look up maps. Imagine needing to find a restaurant or store and not being able to look it up on a smartphone. Instead, you would have to flip through a big book called the Yellow Pages! Before smartphones existed, Elon created Zip2 so that people could look up locations online. That's what Zip2 was all about. The company planned to offer this service to newspapers, which could add the Zip2 maps and business directories to their own websites. Back then, this was a revolutionary idea, as many newspapers hadn't yet embraced the digital world.

At first, the company was small, and Elon and Kimbal worked tirelessly to make it grow. They rented a small office in Palo Alto, California, which is in the heart of Silicon Valley — the place where many of the world's biggest technology companies got their start. The office wasn't fancy, and the brothers didn't have a big team or a lot of money. Elon worked day and night coding the website himself. He often stayed up late into the night, programming and making sure everything worked just right.

Despite these humble beginnings, Zip2 started to attract attention. It wasn't long before they landed contracts with some big names, like *The New York Times* and the *Chicago Tribune*. These newspapers were two of the biggest in the country, and getting them on board was a major win for Elon and his team. Zip2 was growing, and it seemed like the company was on its way to becoming a big success.

However, there were also challenges along the way. As the company expanded, Elon and his brother Kimbal wanted to keep control of the direction it was going in. But Zip2 had a board of directors, which is a group of people who help make decisions for a company. Elon and Kimbal wanted to keep Zip2 independent, but the board had other ideas. At one point, the board wanted to merge Zip2 with another company called CitySearch, which offered a similar service. Elon didn't think this was a good idea, and he managed to convince the board to abandon the merger. This was a victory for Elon, but it wasn't the last time he would face challenges from the people running his company.

Elon's ambition didn't stop at coding and growing the business. He wanted to become the CEO of Zip2, the leader of the company he had helped create. But the board of directors didn't think Elon was ready for that kind of responsibility. Even though Elon had done much of the hard work to build Zip2, the board blocked his attempt to become CEO. This was a tough moment for Elon, but he didn't give up. Instead, he kept working hard, and eventually, his efforts paid off.

In 1999, when Elon was twenty-eight years old, a computer company called Compaq made an offer to buy

Zip2. They offered a huge sum of money — $307 million in cash. This was a massive deal, and it made Elon and his team very wealthy. For Elon's seven percent share in the company, he received $22 million. This was a life-changing amount of money, but for Elon, it was just the beginning. He wasn't interested in simply enjoying his fortune; he had even bigger dreams to chase.

After Compaq bought Zip2, they integrated its software into their services, but the product itself didn't last long. Within a few years, Zip2 was canceled, and Compaq itself was eventually acquired by HP (Hewlett-Packard) in 2002. Despite Zip2 not having a long-term impact, the sale was still a huge success for Elon and his team, giving him the financial boost and experience he needed to pursue even bigger ventures.

With some of the money from selling Zip2, Elon co-founded a new company in March 1999. The company was called X.com, and it was one of the first online banks. At the time, the idea of doing banking over the Internet was still new and a little scary for some people, but Elon saw the potential. He believed that people would soon be using the Internet for all sorts of financial transactions, and he wanted to be at the forefront of this change.

X.com offered online financial services and email payments, allowing people to send money to one another over the Internet. In its first few months, X.com quickly grew to over 200,000 customers, making it one of the fastest-growing online banks of its time. The idea of being able to pay for things and send money without needing to visit a bank in person was groundbreaking, and Elon's company was leading the charge.

One funny thing about X.com was its name. Some of Elon's friends were worried that people might confuse

X.com with a website for something inappropriate, but Elon didn't mind. He liked the name because it was simple, easy to remember, and cool. He even thought that having an email address like "e@x.com" was a fun idea. While the name might have caused a few chuckles, X.com was serious business.

Even though Elon founded X.com, not everything went smoothly. Some of the investors in the company thought Elon was too inexperienced to lead such an important venture. By the end of 1999, they brought in a new CEO to take over leadership of the company, replacing Elon. It was another setback for him, but once again, Elon didn't let it stop him. He stayed involved in the company and kept working to make X.com successful.

In 2000, a major change happened. X.com merged with another company called Confinity. Confinity had developed a service called PayPal, which allowed people to transfer money to each other over the Internet. PayPal was quickly becoming more popular than X.com's own email payment service, and merging the two companies made sense. After the companies merged, the combined entity was named PayPal, reflecting the strength of Confinity's brand. Elon became CEO of the newly formed company, and things seemed to be going well as they navigated the growing online payment market.

In 2000, Elon's life was changing in more ways than just his business ventures. That same year, at the age of twenty-nine, he married Canadian author Justine Wilson, who was twenty-eight at the time. They had met while attending Queen's University in Ontario. Their marriage marked the beginning of a new chapter in Elon's personal life, even as his career continued to grow and evolve.

But soon, challenges in the company arose. Elon preferred using Microsoft-based software to run the company's systems, while many of the company's engineers preferred a different system called Unix. This disagreement led to tension within the company, and one of the co-founders of Confinity, Peter Thiel, decided to leave because of the differences. Eventually, the board of directors decided to remove Elon as CEO once again, replacing him with Peter Thiel, who returned to the company.

Under Peter Thiel's leadership, the company shifted its focus entirely to PayPal, which was becoming the most popular online payment service in the world. In 2001, the company officially changed its name to PayPal. Even though Elon was no longer CEO, he still owned a significant amount of stock in the company and was its largest shareholder, holding about 11.7% of the shares.

In 2002, PayPal was sold to eBay, one of the biggest online marketplaces in the world at that time, for $1.5 billion in stock. Elon's share of the company was worth $176 million, making him even wealthier than before. Despite being removed as CEO twice, Elon had played a crucial role in building PayPal into a successful company.

In 2002, while Elon was experiencing great success in his career, his personal life was touched by tragedy. Elon and Justine welcomed their first child, a baby boy named Nevada Alexander. However, when Nevada was only ten weeks old, something heartbreaking happened — he passed away from sudden infant death syndrome (SIDS), a tragic and unexplained condition where an otherwise healthy baby suddenly dies, usually during sleep, with no clear reason. Despite advances in medicine, doctors still don't fully understand why it happens, making it one of the most devastating occurrences in infants. This was a very difficult time for Elon and Justine, but they were determined to continue building their family. They decided to use a medical process called in vitro fertilization (IVF) to help them have more children in the future. IVF is a process where doctors take an egg from the mother and sperm from the father and put them together in a special lab to create a baby. Once the egg and sperm are combined and start to grow, the doctors place it back in the mother's body to continue growing naturally, like in a regular pregnancy.

They used this method because sometimes couples have trouble getting pregnant in the usual way. There can be different reasons why it's harder for them, so IVF helps by making sure the egg and sperm meet in the best way possible to create a baby. This method gave them a better chance of having more children.

Despite the sadness of losing their first son, Nevada, Elon and Justine were determined to keep moving forward and continue building their family. The experience showed their resilience, a trait that Elon would carry into all areas of his life, including his work. Just as they used IVF to grow their family, Elon always sought ways to overcome obstacles and keep chasing his dreams.

This resilience was also reflected in Elon's connection to his early ventures. Even years after the sale of X.com, Elon still felt a strong attachment to the company. In 2017, more than fifteen years after the company had been sold and transformed into PayPal, Elon bought back the domain name X.com. Although he didn't plan to use the website for anything specific at the time, he said he bought it for "sentimental value," because it reminded him of his early days as an entrepreneur — just like his personal experiences had shaped his determination in other parts of his life.

Elon's experiences with Zip2, X.com and PayPal taught him many important lessons about business, technology, and leadership. He learned that even when things don't go exactly as planned, it's important to keep pushing forward. Each time Elon faced a setback, whether it was being blocked from becoming CEO or being removed from his own company, he didn't let it stop him from dreaming big and working hard.

These early successes gave Elon the money and confidence to take on even bigger challenges in the future. With PayPal behind him, Elon began thinking about the next steps in his journey. He had always been passionate about space exploration, clean energy, and building technology that could make the world a better place. Now, with the resources and experience he had gained, Elon was ready to take the next leap toward achieving his most ambitious dreams.

FOUR

SpaceX: Reaching for the Stars

In the early 2000s, Elon Musk had already built a reputation for being a visionary entrepreneur. He had made a fortune from his earlier ventures like Zip2 and PayPal, but Elon's dreams didn't stop with software and online payments. He had always been fascinated by space and the possibility of humans exploring other planets, particularly Mars. Elon believed that the future of humanity depended on becoming a "multi-planetary species" — in other words, humans needed to live on more than just Earth to survive in the long run. This big idea set him on a path that would change space exploration forever.

In 2001, Elon got involved with an organization called the Mars Society, a nonprofit group that promotes the exploration and settlement of Mars. The Mars Society was interested in getting people excited about the possibility of sending humans to Mars, and Elon was eager to help. He even thought about funding a project that would place a greenhouse full of plants on Mars to show that life could exist there. This idea got Elon thinking more seriously about how humans could one day live on Mars.

To make his plan a reality, Elon needed a way to get things into space. Rockets, of course, are the only way to send objects into space, and Elon knew he needed a rocket to launch his Mars greenhouse project. But instead of building his own rocket from scratch right away, Elon thought he could buy one that was already built. So, in late 2001, he traveled to Moscow, Russia, with two of his friends, Jim Cantrell and Adeo Ressi. They were hoping to buy refurbished intercontinental ballistic missiles (ICBMs) — which are powerful rockets that can launch objects into space.

Elon and his team met with several Russian companies that specialized in rockets, including NPO Lavochkin and Kosmotras. However, when they arrived in Moscow, the companies didn't take Elon seriously. They saw him as a beginner in the space industry, someone who didn't really know what he was doing. Because of this, Elon left Russia empty-handed, without the rocket he had hoped to buy.

But Elon wasn't ready to give up. In February 2002, he and his team returned to Russia, this time with Mike Griffin, the president of In-Q-Tel, who had experience in the space industry. They met with Kosmotras again and were offered one rocket for $8 million. Even though Elon had plenty of money from his previous successes, he felt this price was way too high. He believed that rockets could be made for much less. So, instead of buying the overpriced rocket, Elon made a bold decision: he was going to start his own company to build rockets at a lower cost. This decision would eventually lead to the creation of SpaceX.

In May 2002, Elon officially founded SpaceX (short for Space Exploration Technologies Corp). He invested $100 million of his own money into the company and became both the CEO and chief engineer. Elon's goal was simple but incredibly ambitious: to make space travel more affordable and to eventually help humans live on Mars.

Starting a rocket company wasn't easy, even for someone as smart and determined as Elon. Building rockets is extremely complicated, and it requires a lot of money, time, and expertise. But Elon believed that SpaceX could make rockets cheaper by designing them to be reusable. Most rockets are only used once — they launch into space, and the parts that don't burn up fall into the ocean, never to be used again. This makes space travel very expensive. Elon's idea was to build rockets that could be used over and over, like airplanes. If SpaceX could figure out how to reuse rockets, it would make space travel much more affordable.

Starting a rocket company wasn't the only exciting thing happening in Elon's life during these years. His family was also growing! In 2004, Elon and his wife Justine welcomed two new members to their family — twins named Griffin and Xavier. The birth of the twins was a joyful moment, and Elon and Justine were thrilled to become parents to two energetic boys. At this time, the Musk family was living in California, where Elon was busy working on his ventures, including SpaceX and Tesla.

But their family didn't stop there. Just two years later, in 2006, they were blessed again — this time with triplets! The triplets, Kai, Saxon, and Damian, brought even more energy and joy to the Musk household. Suddenly, their family was filled with the happy chaos of five boys. Their home in California was now bustling with activity, as Elon balanced his work as an entrepreneur and his growing role as a father.

As Elon's family expanded, so did his ambitions with SpaceX. The company's first rocket, the Falcon 1, represented a huge leap forward in Elon's dream of making space travel more affordable. SpaceX began as a small startup, and like many startups, it faced significant challenges. At the beginning, around 160 people worked for SpaceX, most of them engineers, scientists, and technicians. They were based in a humble set of buildings in El Segundo, California, close to Los Angeles International Airport. The buildings were mostly industrial warehouses, filled with labs and manufacturing areas where the team could build and test rocket parts.

Elon was deeply involved in every aspect of the project. Not only was he the founder and CEO, but he also acted as the chief engineer. This meant that he worked closely with his team on the design, development, and problem-solving processes. Elon spent long hours at the office and would often roll up his sleeves to dive into technical issues, from engine design to material choices. His hands-on leadership style pushed the team to work incredibly hard, even as they faced setbacks.

The team's hard work and dedication were put to the test in 2006, the same year Elon's triplets were born, when SpaceX attempted its first launch of the Falcon 1. However, despite the excitement and effort that went into the mission, the rocket failed to reach orbit and malfunctioned during launch. The failure was due to a problem with one of the rocket's fuel lines, which caused the engine to shut down prematurely. This technical issue prevented the Falcon 1 from gaining enough speed and altitude to reach space. This was a major disappointment, but Elon and his team didn't give up. They kept working on improving the Falcon 1, learning from their mistakes, and trying again.

Later that year, even though SpaceX had not yet successfully launched a rocket, they were awarded a contract by NASA (National Aeronautics and Space Administration). NASA had just started a new program called the Commercial Orbital Transportation Services (COTS) program, which aimed to work with private companies to deliver cargo to space. The contract gave SpaceX some much-needed funding to continue working on their rockets.

However, things didn't get easier right away. SpaceX tried launching the Falcon 1 two more times, and both attempts failed. The second launch in 2007 failed due to a fuel leak, which caused the rocket to spin out of control just a few minutes after liftoff. Then, in 2008, during the third launch, the first stage of the rocket collided with the second stage during separation, leading to another failure. By this point, Elon was running out of money. He had invested most of his fortune into SpaceX, and if the next launch didn't succeed, the company might have to shut down. Elon's other company, Tesla, which was focused on electric cars, was also struggling at the same time. It was a difficult period for Elon, and he was close to losing everything.

Then, in 2008, SpaceX made history. On their fourth attempt, the Falcon 1 rocket successfully reached orbit, making it the first privately developed liquid-fueled rocket to do so. This was a huge achievement for SpaceX and for Elon. After years of hard work and several failures, they had finally proved that SpaceX could build rockets that worked. This success came just in time to save the company from financial ruin.

Later that same year, SpaceX received another massive contract from NASA. This time, it was for $1.6 billion, and it was for twelve flights of SpaceX's larger rocket, the Falcon 9, along with its Dragon spacecraft. Each flight would use a different Dragon spacecraft, as at that time, SpaceX had not yet fully developed the capability for reusing spacecraft for multiple missions. However, the goal was to make both the Falcon 9 rocket and the Dragon spacecraft reusable in the future, which SpaceX later achieved with significant advancements in rocket and spacecraft recovery and refurbishment technology. In short, Falcon 9 and Dragon spacecraft were to be used to deliver cargo to the International Space Station (ISS), replacing the Space Shuttle, which was set to retire in 2011. The ISS is a large space station that orbits Earth and serves as a home and research laboratory for astronauts from different countries. It is where scientists conduct experiments in space to learn more about things like how humans can live in space and how space affects various scientific processes. Their Space Shuttle had been NASA's main vehicle for sending astronauts and cargo into space since its first flight in 1981.

It was unique because it was reusable — after launching into space, it could return to Earth and land like an airplane. However, by 2011, the Space Shuttle was aging and becoming too expensive to maintain, so NASA needed a new way to send supplies to the ISS. That's where SpaceX and their Falcon 9 rocket came in, offering a more affordable and efficient solution. This contract was a major turning point for SpaceX, giving them the financial stability to keep developing their rockets and spacecraft.

In 2012, SpaceX made history again. Their Falcon 9 rocket launched the Dragon spacecraft, which successfully docked with the International Space Station, making it the first commercial spacecraft to do so. This achievement was groundbreaking, as it showed that private companies like SpaceX could play a major role in space exploration. Until that point, only government space agencies like NASA or Russia's space program had been able to send spacecraft to the ISS. Now, SpaceX was proving that private companies could also take on these big challenges.

But Elon and SpaceX weren't just focused on sending cargo to space. From the beginning, Elon had always dreamed of making rockets reusable. If SpaceX could build rockets that could land back on Earth after launching, they could be used again, saving a lot of money. After years of development, SpaceX finally achieved this goal in 2015. They successfully landed the first stage of their Falcon 9 rocket back on Earth at Cape Canaveral, Florida, after a mission. This was a major step toward making space travel more affordable. Instead of letting the rocket fall into the ocean and be destroyed, SpaceX had figured out how to land it safely so it could be used again.

After that first successful landing, SpaceX continued to improve their rocket landings. They even started landing rockets on platforms in the Atlantic Ocean, called autonomous spaceport drone ships. These ships were essentially floating landing pads that allowed SpaceX to recover rockets even when they were launched far out over the ocean. With each successful landing, SpaceX was getting closer to making reusable rockets a reality.

In 2018, SpaceX achieved another milestone with the launch of the Falcon Heavy, their most powerful rocket yet. The Falcon Heavy was designed to carry heavy payloads into space, and its first mission had a very special cargo — Elon's own Tesla Roadster, an electric sports car! The car was placed inside the rocket and launched into space as a fun demonstration of what the Falcon Heavy could do. This launch was a huge success, and it showed that SpaceX was capable of launching massive payloads into space, opening the door to even more ambitious missions.

While all of this was happening, SpaceX was also working on something even bigger: a new rocket called Starship. Starship was designed to be fully reusable and capable of carrying large numbers of people and cargo to distant planets like Mars. Elon's dream of helping humans live on other planets was closer than ever with the development of Starship. SpaceX began testing early versions of Starship in 2019, and while there were still challenges to overcome, the company was making progress toward this ambitious goal.

In 2020, SpaceX reached yet another major milestone: they launched their first crewed flight. Called the Demo-2 mission, this flight marked the first time a private company had ever sent astronauts into orbit and successfully attached a crewed spacecraft with the International Space Station. Essentially, SpaceX's Crew Dragon acted like a "space taxi," safely carrying astronauts to the ISS, where they joined the crew aboard the orbiting station. This was a historic achievement, as it proved that private companies like SpaceX could safely send people into space, something that had only been done by government agencies like NASA before.

Elon's dream of making space travel more affordable and helping humanity explore the stars was becoming a reality. Through SpaceX, he has transformed the space industry and shown that private companies could play a major role in space exploration. From the early days of trying to buy rockets in Russia to building reusable rockets and sending astronauts into space, Elon's journey with SpaceX has been full of challenges and triumphs.

As SpaceX continues to develop new technology, including the Starship rocket, Elon's ultimate goal of helping humans live on Mars gets closer and closer. Elon often talks about Mars as the "next frontier" for humanity. He envisions a future where people are living and working on Mars, just like they do on Earth. He believes that it's possible to create a city on Mars, complete with homes, schools, and businesses, and he's determined to make this vision a reality. But why Mars? Of all the planets in the solar system, Mars is the most similar to Earth in terms of its size, gravity, and day length. While it's much colder and lacks the oxygen we need to breathe, Elon believes that technology can help overcome these challenges.

To make Mars livable for humans, SpaceX would need to send supplies and equipment long before the first people arrive. This could include things like machines that create breathable air, water systems, and habitats where astronauts could live. Elon has even suggested the idea of "terraforming" Mars — which means transforming the planet's environment to make it more like Earth so humans could live there more easily. One of the boldest ideas he's mentioned is using nuclear bombs to heat up the planet's atmosphere. The basic idea is that detonating these bombs near the poles of Mars could release enough heat to melt the ice caps, creating water vapor and thickening the atmosphere, which might help warm the planet. However, this idea is very controversial. Many scientists have pointed out that it could have unpredictable consequences, and there are still many challenges to making Mars a place where humans could live. While it's just one of many possible solutions, it's an example of Elon's ambitious thinking when it comes to exploring and possibly colonizing other planets.

Elon has always been clear that the journey to Mars won't be easy. The distance between Earth and Mars varies depending on their orbits, but on average, the planets are about 140 million miles apart (225 million kilometers). A trip to Mars would take around six months each way, meaning that astronauts would need to be well-prepared for a long and difficult journey. Once they arrive, they'll face other challenges, like the planet's thin atmosphere, extreme cold, and radiation from the Sun. But Elon believes that with the right technology, all of these problems can be solved.

In addition to the technical challenges, Elon knows that getting people excited about space is just as important. He believes that space exploration is an adventure that can inspire the next generation of scientists, engineers, and dreamers. That's one of the reasons he launched his own Tesla Roadster into space aboard the Falcon Heavy. The car, with a dummy astronaut in the driver's seat, is now orbiting the Sun, serving as a reminder that space is not just for astronauts — it's for everyone who dares to dream.

Elon's vision for Mars and beyond is about more than just technology. It's about the future of humanity. He often talks about how life on Earth is fragile, and how having humans live on other planets could protect us from disasters, like an asteroid hitting Earth or a major environmental crisis. By creating a civilization on Mars, Elon believes that humans could ensure their survival, no matter what happens on our home planet.

Another challenge is getting people to Mars safely. Space is a harsh and dangerous environment, and while SpaceX has made great progress, there's still a lot of work to be done to make sure that astronauts can survive the journey and thrive once they arrive. Elon is realistic about the risks, and he has even said that the first people to go to Mars will face serious dangers. But he's confident that with determination and innovation, humans will eventually succeed.

Of course, there are many critics of Elon's Mars plans. Some people argue that the money and resources being spent on space exploration could be better used to solve problems on Earth, like poverty, climate change, or healthcare. Elon acknowledges these concerns but believes that space exploration and solving Earth's problems can go hand in hand. In fact, some of the technology developed for space missions could directly help address issues on our planet, like clean energy and water purification.

The story of SpaceX is a testament to Elon's determination, creativity, and belief in the power of technology to solve big problems. With each new achievement, SpaceX reaches further into the stars, and the possibilities for the future of space exploration become more exciting than ever.

FIVE

Tesla Motors: Driving into the Future

Elon Musk's journey with Tesla Motors began not long after he founded SpaceX. While his goal with SpaceX was to make space travel affordable and eventually help humans reach Mars, his vision for Tesla was focused on something a bit closer to home — making transportation on Earth more sustainable. The idea of building electric cars wasn't new, but Elon believed that electric vehicles could be faster, cooler, and more efficient than the gasoline-powered cars people had been driving for over a century. With Tesla Motors, Elon was ready to lead the charge into the future of clean, electric transportation.

Tesla Motors, now known simply as Tesla, was actually founded in 2003 by two engineers, Martin Eberhard and Marc Tarpenning. These two men had the idea to create electric cars that could challenge the traditional gasoline-powered vehicles that dominated the market. They wanted to prove that electric cars could be powerful, fast, and exciting. However, they needed money to get their idea off the ground, and that's where Elon came in.

In early 2004, Elon joined Tesla Motors as a major investor. He led the company's first round of funding, investing over $6 million of his own money. This made him the largest shareholder in the company, owning approximately 28% of Tesla's shares at the time. Even though Elon wasn't the original founder, his investment and belief in the company's vision gave him a major role in its development. Elon became the chairman of the board, which meant he had a say in the big decisions Tesla made. Although he wasn't involved in the day-to-day operations at first, Elon made sure to play a key role in designing Tesla's first car, the Roadster.

The Roadster was a very special car. Released in 2008, it wasn't just any electric vehicle — it was a sleek, sporty, and fast car that could go from zero to sixty miles (about ninety-six kilometers) per hour in under four seconds. Most people didn't think electric cars could be that exciting, but the Roadster proved them wrong. It was the first all-electric sports car to use lithium-ion batteries, which are the same kind of batteries that power laptops and smartphones. The Roadster could drive over 200 miles (322 kilometers) on a single charge, which was an incredible achievement for an electric car at the time. Tesla sold about 2,500 Roadsters, primarily in the United States. The car was marketed as a luxury sports vehicle and was available in cities like Los Angeles, San Francisco, and New York, where there was a strong interest in innovation and sustainable technology. The Roadster came with a high price tag, costing around $109,000, making it a car for people who wanted both performance and to be part of the green movement.

However, Tesla's early days weren't without challenges. Even though the idea of creating electric vehicles was exciting, the road to success was anything but smooth. The company faced significant financial problems right from the start. Designing and building electric cars required a lot of money, and Tesla was burning through cash faster than expected. There were also disagreements among the leadership team about how the company should move forward. These disagreements created tension at Tesla, especially between Elon Musk and Martin Eberhard, one of the original founders of the company. Eberhard had his own vision for Tesla, but it often clashed with Elon's ideas, leading to a series of conflicts about the direction of the company.

Martin saw Tesla as a company that should focus on building niche electric sports cars for a wealthy market. He believed that starting with a high-end vehicle, like the Roadster, would generate attention and revenue. His idea was to keep Tesla small and focused on perfecting electric sports cars before moving on to more affordable vehicles. He also emphasized steady, gradual growth and careful engineering. On the other hand, Elon had much bigger ambitions for Tesla. He didn't just want Tesla to be a niche car company; he wanted it to revolutionize the entire automotive industry by producing electric vehicles for the mass market. His goal was to create affordable electric cars that could replace gasoline-powered vehicles worldwide. Musk pushed for faster innovation, higher production rates, and a more aggressive timeline to bring electric cars to the mainstream. He was willing to take more risks to achieve this vision, including taking on significant financial challenges and moving quickly with development.

In 2007, after months of disputes and growing frustration, Martin Eberhard was forced to leave the company. His departure marked a big shift for Tesla, as one of its key founders was no longer part of the leadership team. This wasn't an easy decision for Tesla, but it became clear that the company needed a new direction if it was going to survive. Elon Musk, who had been serving as chairman of the board, decided to step in and take a more active role in leading the company.

The very next year, in 2008, Elon officially became the CEO of Tesla. While this was a big moment for the company, it also marked a challenging time in Elon's personal life. That same year, Elon and his wife Justine decided to divorce after eight years of marriage. It was a difficult time for both of them, but they remained committed to co-parenting and shared custody of their five children. Even though the divorce added emotional strain, Elon continued to balance his responsibilities as a father alongside his growing professional commitments.

While navigating these personal challenges, Elon's role as CEO came during one of the toughest periods in Tesla's history. The world was in the middle of the financial crisis of 2008, a time when many companies around the globe were struggling to stay afloat. People were losing their jobs, businesses were going bankrupt, and investors were hesitant to put money into risky ventures like electric cars.

For a young company like Tesla, the financial crisis made it even harder to raise the money needed to keep developing their cars. Despite everything happening in his personal and professional life, Elon remained committed to Tesla's mission and was determined to steer the company through these tough times.

At the same time, Elon was also juggling the challenges of running SpaceX, which was facing its own financial struggles. Both companies were at risk of collapsing, and Elon was under immense pressure. To make things even harder, Tesla's car production was facing delays, and they were running out of money to pay their employees and suppliers. Some people even predicted that Tesla wouldn't survive much longer.

Elon later revealed that Tesla was just three days away from running out of cash when, on Christmas Eve, they received a last-minute $40 million investment from existing investors and shareholders. This critical infusion of funds provided a lifeline that allowed the company to survive at the very last moment. The close call came at a time when Tesla was struggling to ramp up production of its electric cars, while facing immense financial pressure, but this crucial investment helped keep the company afloat and on the path to success.

Despite these incredibly tough times, Elon never gave up. He was deeply committed to Tesla's mission of creating electric vehicles and pushing the world toward a future with cleaner transportation. Elon believed that electric cars were the solution to many of the world's environmental problems, and he was determined to make Tesla a success, no matter how difficult the road ahead was.

To keep Tesla alive, Elon made a huge personal sacrifice. He invested much of his own money into the company, using the fortune he had earned from the sale of PayPal to fund Tesla's operations. This wasn't just a small investment — Elon put nearly all of his remaining cash into the company to keep it going. He took an enormous risk, betting everything he had on Tesla's future. It was a bold move, and it showed how much Elon believed in Tesla's potential.

As CEO, Elon worked day and night to turn Tesla around. He was involved in every part of the company, from designing the cars to solving production issues. Elon wasn't just a figurehead — he was a hands-on leader who made sure every detail was perfect. His dedication and hard work began to pay off, and slowly, Tesla started to get back on its feet. The company pushed forward with the development of the Model S, which would go on to become one of the most successful electric cars in the world.

With Elon as the CEO, Tesla began to focus not just on sports cars like the Roadster, but also on cars that more people could afford. In 2012, Tesla released the Model S, a four-door electric sedan. The base price for the 2012 Model S started at $60,890, but higher-performance versions, like the Performance Sedan and the Signature Performance Sedan, could cost as much as $100,000, depending on the features and specifications. The Model S was a game-changer for the electric car industry. It wasn't just fast and stylish — it was also packed with advanced technology. It had a large touchscreen in the center console, which allowed drivers to control almost everything in the car, from navigation to entertainment. The Model S could also drive long distances on a single charge, with some versions able to go over 300 miles (483 kilometers) before needing to recharge.

The Model S quickly became popular, earning awards and praise for its performance and design. It proved that electric cars could be more than just a niche product — they could compete with the best gasoline-powered cars in the world. The success of the Model S helped Tesla grow and build its reputation as a leader in the electric vehicle industry.

Tesla didn't stop with the Model S. In 2015, the company introduced the Model X, a crossover SUV. The Tesla Model X had a starting price of around $80,000 at launch for the base model, while more premium versions could reach over $100,000, depending on features. The Model X was unique not just because it was electric, but also because of its futuristic features, like the "falcon-wing" doors that opened upward instead of out to the sides. This made the Model X stand out from any other SUV on the market. It was designed to be a family-friendly vehicle that was also fast and environmentally friendly. Like the Model S, the Model X could travel long distances on a single charge and had plenty of room for passengers and cargo.

Elon's goal wasn't just to make high-end electric cars, though. He wanted to make electric cars affordable for everyone. That's why, in 2017, Tesla released the Model 3, a mass-market sedan that was priced lower than the Model S and Model X. The Model 3 was designed to be Tesla's most affordable car, starting at around $35,000. It quickly became a huge success, with hundreds of thousands of people placing orders before the car was even released. By 2020, the Model 3 had become the all-time best-selling electric car in the world, selling over one million units globally. It showed that electric cars weren't just for wealthy people — they were for everyone.

As Tesla continued to grow, it introduced more vehicles. In 2020, the company launched the Model Y, a crossover similar to the Model X but more affordable. The Tesla Model Y was available at various price points depending on the version. The Standard Range variant was priced around $39,000 at launch, making it more affordable compared to other models like the Model X. The Long Range variant cost around $52,990, and the high-performance version of the Model Y was priced at about $60,990. These options allowed Tesla to cater to a wider range of customers, making the Model Y a popular choice for those looking for an electric vehicle with SUV-like functionality at different price points. Like the Model 3, the Model Y became incredibly popular, and by December 2023, it had become the best-selling vehicle of any kind, not just electric cars. This was a huge milestone for Tesla, as it showed that electric vehicles were now mainstream.

In addition to making electric cars, Tesla also started working on other projects related to clean energy. Elon believed that the future of transportation and energy should be sustainable, meaning it wouldn't harm the planet. To help make this vision a reality, Tesla began building massive factories called Gigafactories. The first Gigafactory, Gigafactory 1, was built in Sparks, Nevada, in partnership with Panasonic and was set to eventually employ around 10,000 people once fully operational. These factories were designed to produce not only electric vehicles but also lithium-ion batteries, which are the key to making electric cars run. By building batteries on a large scale, Tesla could lower the cost of electric cars and make them more accessible to people around the world.

Tesla also got involved in developing energy storage systems for homes and businesses. The company's Powerwall and Powerpack products allow people to store electricity generated from solar panels, making it possible for them to power their homes with clean energy even when the sun isn't shining. This was another way Tesla was helping to reduce the world's reliance on fossil fuels and promote renewable energy.

One of the most exciting things Tesla has worked on in recent years is the Cybertruck, an all-electric pickup truck that looks like something straight out of a science fiction movie. The Cybertruck was unveiled in 2019, and its futuristic design immediately got people talking. Unlike traditional pickup trucks, the Cybertruck is built with an ultra-hard stainless steel body and armored glass. It's designed to be tough, durable, and capable of handling any job, all while being fully electric. Tesla began delivering the first Cybertrucks in November 2023, and the truck is already making waves in the automotive world. Tesla's Cybertruck launched at different price points depending on the model. The standard all-wheel-drive version started at $79,990, while the high-end tri-motor Cyberbeast version was priced at $99,990.

Tesla's journey has been marked by incredible achievements, but it hasn't always been smooth sailing. The company faced challenges along the way, from financial difficulties to production delays. However, under Elon's leadership, Tesla has continued to push the boundaries of what's possible in the world of electric vehicles. Elon even gave himself the playful title of "Technoking" in 2021 while still serving as the CEO of the company, showing his unique sense of humor and his belief in the power of technology to shape the future.

One of the most important milestones in Tesla's history was its initial public offering (IPO) in 2010. This was when Tesla became a publicly traded company, meaning people could buy shares of Tesla stock. Over the years, Tesla's stock price rose significantly, and by 2020, Tesla had become the most valuable carmaker in the world, surpassing traditional giants like Toyota and General Motors. When Tesla went public in 2010, the initial stock price was seventeen dollars per share. Over the years, as Tesla continued to innovate and release new electric vehicles, its stock price surged significantly. By 2020, Tesla's stock had risen dramatically, reaching around $705 per share. In 2021, Tesla's market value reached $1 trillion, making it one of only a handful of companies in the world to achieve this level of success.

Elon's involvement with Tesla hasn't been without controversy, though. In 2021, he proposed on Twitter that he should sell ten percent of his Tesla stock, following public debates about wealthy individuals and taxes. After over three million people voted in favor of the idea on Twitter, Elon sold billions of dollars' worth of Tesla stock by the end of the year. His decision to sell the stock led to investigations by the Securities and Exchange Commission (SEC) to ensure everything was done legally. The Securities and Exchange Commission (SEC) is a U.S. government agency responsible for regulating the stock market and protecting investors. It ensures that companies and individuals follow legal and ethical practices when buying, selling, or trading stocks and other financial assets. The SEC also investigates any actions that might involve fraud or insider trading, ensuring that the stock market operates fairly and transparently. Despite these challenges, Elon remained focused on Tesla's mission and continued to lead the company toward new heights.

In addition to building cars and batteries, Tesla has also been working on developing robots. In 2022, Elon unveiled Optimus, a robot that Tesla is designing to help with various tasks, from manufacturing to household chores. While Optimus is still in development, Elon believes that robots like it could play an important role in the future, helping people with everyday tasks and improving efficiency in industries. Imagine how exciting it would be to have robots assisting with daily chores at home or helping factories run more smoothly — this could completely change the way we live and work, making life easier and more efficient for everyone!

Tesla's influence is now reaching far beyond the United States. In 2023, Elon met with the Prime Minister of India, Narendra Modi, to discuss the possibility of investing in the country. Elon is eager to expand Tesla's presence globally, and India, with its large population and growing demand for clean energy, is a key market for Tesla's future.

Tesla's main factory, known as the Tesla Gigafactory, is located in Fremont, California. However, the company operates several Gigafactories around the world, including in Nevada, Texas, and Shanghai, China. These factories produce electric vehicles, batteries, and other components essential to Tesla's operations. As of 2023, Tesla has expanded its workforce significantly, employing over 127,000 people globally. This global reach helps Tesla meet the growing demand for electric vehicles and clean energy solutions across various markets, including the U.S., Europe, and Asia.

From the Roadster to the Model Y, and from electric cars to robots, Tesla has come a long way since its early days. Under Elon Musk's leadership, the company has revolutionized the automotive industry and shown the world that electric vehicles are not just the future — they are the present.

SIX

SolarCity: Powering the World with Clean Energy

When Elon Musk took on the challenge of building electric cars with Tesla, he didn't stop thinking about how he could make the world cleaner and greener. His vision wasn't just about cars; he wanted to transform how people got their energy too. Elon believed that the future of energy should be sustainable, meaning it should come from sources that don't harm the planet. One of the best ways to do that, he thought, was by using the sun. The sun is an incredible source of power, and it provides more than enough energy to power the whole world if people could find ways to capture and use it effectively.

In 2006, Elon helped create a company called SolarCity to make this dream of solar energy a reality. The idea for SolarCity came from Elon, but he didn't start the company himself. Instead, his cousins, Lyndon and Peter Rive, took Elon's concept and built the company, while Elon provided the financial backing to get things going. SolarCity's mission was simple but ambitious: to make it easier and cheaper for people to put solar panels on their homes and businesses, so they could generate their own clean energy from the sun.

Solar panels, which capture sunlight and turn it into electricity, had been around for many years, but they were still expensive and difficult to install. Most people didn't know much about how they worked, and they weren't sure if solar energy was a good option for them. SolarCity wanted to change that by making the process easy, affordable, and appealing. They offered people the chance to install solar panels with little or no upfront cost, and instead, they could pay for the solar energy they used over time. This business model helped SolarCity grow quickly because it made solar energy accessible to more people.

By 2013, SolarCity had become one of the biggest providers of solar power systems in the United States. In fact, it was the second-largest company of its kind. They installed solar panels on thousands of homes, businesses, and government buildings, helping people save money on their energy bills while reducing their reliance on fossil fuels like coal and natural gas, which pollute the environment.

But Elon and SolarCity didn't just want to stop at making solar energy available for individual homes and businesses. They had much bigger plans. In 2014, Elon promoted the idea of building a massive solar panel factory in Buffalo, New York. This factory would be triple the size of the largest solar plant in the United States at the time, and it would allow SolarCity to produce more advanced solar panels at a lower cost. This would make solar energy even more affordable for everyone.

Construction of this enormous factory, known as the "Gigafactory," began in 2014. The factory was built to not only produce solar panels but also to help SolarCity develop new technology to improve the efficiency of these panels. Solar panels work by capturing sunlight and converting it into electricity, but like any technology, they can always be made better. The more efficient the panels are, the more energy they can produce from the same amount of sunlight, which makes solar power even more useful.

The Gigafactory in Buffalo was completed in 2017, and it operated in partnership with Panasonic, a company known for making electronics and batteries. This partnership helped SolarCity produce high-quality solar panels at the scale needed to supply the growing demand for clean energy. However, this partnership with Panasonic ended in early 2020 as Tesla, which had acquired SolarCity (back in 2016), decided to take over full control of the operations at the Gigafactory in Buffalo. As Tesla's ambitions and capabilities in clean energy grew, the company wanted to manage the entire production process itself. By taking full control, Tesla could manage its operations, integrate its solar panel production more closely with its energy storage solutions, and accelerate its plans for expanding solar energy products. This move allowed Tesla to innovate faster, develop new technology, and improve the efficiency of its solar products, all while furthering its goal of becoming a leader in clean energy.

In 2016, something major had happened that would change the direction of SolarCity and Tesla. Elon had proposed that Tesla acquire SolarCity and merge it with Tesla's battery division. This move made sense to Elon because it would allow Tesla to offer both solar panels and batteries together. This combination would help people not only generate clean energy but also store it. Storing energy in batteries is important because the sun doesn't shine all the time, and people need electricity even when it's cloudy or at night. Tesla's batteries, like the Powerwall, could store solar energy during the day so that people could use it whenever they needed it, even after the sun had gone down.

Tesla acquired SolarCity for $2 billion, and the two companies merged together to form Tesla Energy. This new division would focus on creating clean energy solutions for the future, combining Tesla's expertise in batteries with SolarCity's experience in solar power. The idea was to create a complete system where people could generate, store, and use their own renewable energy, reducing their reliance on traditional power grids that rely on polluting fossil fuels.

However, the deal to acquire SolarCity wasn't without controversy, and it stirred up a lot of questions. When Tesla announced that it was buying SolarCity, some people, including many of Tesla's own investors, became worried. SolarCity had been struggling financially, and some thought that buying the company would put Tesla at risk. They wondered if Tesla was taking on too much by adding another company with money problems. In fact, when the deal was made public, Tesla's stock price dropped by more than ten percent because of investor concerns. Some shareholders even went a step further — they filed lawsuits against Elon and Tesla's board of directors. They argued that Elon had pushed Tesla to buy SolarCity for his own benefit, because SolarCity was founded by his cousins, Lyndon and Peter Rive, and Elon himself had invested a lot of money into it. These shareholders believed that the deal wasn't in the best interest of Tesla or its shareholders, and that it was more about helping SolarCity and Elon's family.

This disagreement led to a big court case, where groups of Tesla shareholders claimed the acquisition of SolarCity harmed Tesla's business. They wanted compensation, believing Tesla had lost money because of the purchase. In 2020, most of Tesla's directors settled the case, which meant they agreed to pay money to put an end to the lawsuit without admitting they did anything wrong. But Elon wasn't willing to settle — he believed he had done the right thing and wanted to defend the decision in court. He became the sole defendant in the case and stood firm in his belief that acquiring SolarCity was the best move for Tesla's future.

Two years later, in 2022, Elon finally got his answer when the court ruled in his favor. The court found that Elon hadn't acted improperly, and that the decision to buy SolarCity was made to help Tesla grow and achieve its clean energy mission, not just to benefit Elon personally or his family. This decision was a big win for Elon, as it cleared him of any wrongdoing. This event serves as a great reminder that even when things get tough and people doubt your decisions, standing up for what you believe in can pay off in the end!

Despite the challenges and controversies surrounding the merger, Tesla Energy continued to grow. The combination of solar panels and batteries allowed Tesla to offer complete energy solutions for homes and businesses. Customers could install solar panels on their roofs to capture clean energy from the sun and store that energy in Tesla's Powerwall batteries for use later. This made homes more energy-efficient and less dependent on traditional power grids.

Elon believed that solar energy and battery storage were key to solving one of the world's biggest problems — climate change. Climate change is caused by the buildup of greenhouse gases, like carbon dioxide, in the atmosphere. These gases come from burning fossil fuels like coal, oil, and natural gas, which are used to generate electricity and power vehicles. By switching to renewable energy sources like solar power, which doesn't produce harmful emissions, people could reduce their carbon footprint and help protect the planet.

Tesla Energy also focused on helping businesses and even entire communities make the switch to clean energy. Large solar projects were developed to power schools, factories, and office buildings. In some cases, Tesla's energy systems were used to power entire islands or remote areas where access to traditional energy sources was difficult. For example, Tesla installed solar power and battery systems on the island of Ta'u in American Samoa, a U.S. territory in the South Pacific, allowing the island to run almost entirely on renewable energy.

In addition to solar panels and batteries for homes and businesses, Tesla Energy also developed large-scale battery systems to support the electricity grid. These systems, known as "Powerpacks" and "Megapacks," could store large amounts of energy that could be used to balance the supply and demand of electricity. This was especially helpful in places where power outages were common or where the energy grid relied heavily on fossil fuels. By storing energy during times of low demand and releasing it when needed, Tesla's energy storage systems could help prevent blackouts and reduce the need for dirty energy sources.

One of the most famous examples of this large-scale battery technology was in South Australia. In 2017, after a series of power outages, the South Australian government asked for help from Tesla to stabilize their energy grid. In response, Tesla built the world's largest lithium-ion battery system, known as the "Hornsdale Power Reserve." This massive battery system could store enough energy to power thousands of homes, and it helped prevent future blackouts while supporting the transition to renewable energy in the region.

Through Tesla Energy, Elon's vision of a world powered by clean, renewable energy was starting to take shape. SolarCity had played a big role in bringing solar power to more homes and businesses, and after merging with Tesla, the company expanded its efforts to include energy storage solutions as well. Elon's goal wasn't just to build electric cars or launch rockets into space — he wanted to help create a sustainable future where energy came from the sun, and where people could live without harming the planet.

SolarCity, now fully integrated into Tesla Energy, has expanded its reach across the United States, providing solar panel installations and energy storage solutions. Its headquarters are in San Mateo, California, and it continues to employ thousands of workers across various locations. By 2023, Tesla Energy has grown to employ over 12,000 people, playing a significant role in the transition to renewable energy. This workforce has been crucial in pushing forward Elon Musk's vision of a sustainable future, making clean energy more accessible to homes and businesses.

Looking back, it's clear that SolarCity and Tesla Energy have had a huge impact on the world. While there were bumps along the way, Elon's determination to push for a cleaner, greener future has never wavered. Through innovation, hard work, and the belief that solar energy could change the world, SolarCity and Tesla Energy have helped bring us closer to a future where clean energy powers everything, from homes to businesses to entire communities. The journey to making the world a better place with clean energy is far from over, but Elon and his team at Tesla Energy are well on their way to making that future a reality.

SEVEN

Starlink: Connecting the World from Space

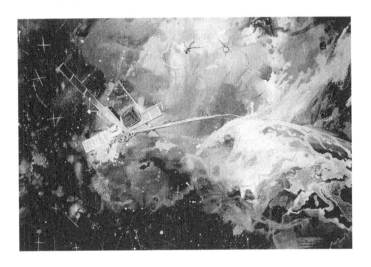

After launching SpaceX and working to make space travel affordable, Elon Musk turned his attention to another big idea: connecting the world with fast and reliable Internet. Elon realized that many parts of the world, especially remote and rural areas, had little or no access to the Internet. In our modern world, Internet access is incredibly important. People use it for school, work, communicating with others, and even for learning about the world. Elon wanted to change that and make the Internet accessible to everyone, no matter where they lived, by using satellites in space. That's how the idea for Starlink was born.

Starlink is a project created by SpaceX to build a network, or constellation, of thousands of small satellites that would orbit the Earth and beam Internet down to the surface. These satellites are different from the ones used by many other satellite Internet companies, which usually place their satellites in high orbits, far from the Earth. Starlink's satellites are placed in low-Earth orbit, meaning they orbit much closer to the planet. This helps make the Internet faster and reduces something called "latency," which is the delay between sending and receiving information online. For people who use the Internet to stream videos, play games, or have video calls, low latency is really important.

In 2015, SpaceX began developing the Starlink project, knowing it would take years to get all the satellites into space and work together. The goal was to launch thousands of satellites over time to create a complete network. The first two prototype satellites, which were like test versions, were launched in February 2018. These early satellites helped SpaceX figure out how to improve the design and make sure everything worked as planned. A second set of test satellites was launched in May 2019, and with that launch, SpaceX began deploying the first large group of operational satellites — sixty in total.

By 2020, Starlink was becoming a reality. SpaceX estimated that the entire project, which would take about a decade to fully complete, would cost around $10 billion. That's a huge amount of money, but Elon believed it was worth it because of how much good it could do. He wanted Starlink to provide high-speed Internet to people in every corner of the globe, especially in places where it was difficult or impossible to lay cables and build traditional Internet networks. For example, people living in faraway villages, on islands, or in remote mountain areas would be able to access the same fast Internet as people in big cities.

Starlink started to roll out its service to early users in 2020, and people were excited. Many people who had never had reliable Internet before were finally able to connect to the web. Farmers in rural areas could use it to get weather updates and manage their crops, students could take online classes, and families could stream movies or talk to friends and relatives across the world. Starlink was changing lives, one satellite at a time.

But while Starlink was helping many people, it also had some critics. Some astronomers, scientists who study space, were concerned that Starlink's satellites were blocking their view of the night sky. The satellites were visible from Earth and could interfere with telescopes and space observations. Groups like the International Astronomical Union, which supports space research, said that having so many satellites in space could make it harder to see stars and planets. SpaceX worked on ways to reduce how much the satellites reflected light, but the issue was still a concern for many.

Another challenge Starlink faced was the risk of space collisions. Since there would be so many satellites orbiting Earth, some people worried that they could crash into each other or other spacecraft! Each Starlink satellite is quite compact, measuring about 9.4 feet (2.9 meters) in length, 4.7 feet (1.4 meters) in width, and weighing around 573 pounds (260 kilograms). These small but numerous satellites orbit at low Earth altitudes, which adds to the complexity of avoiding potential collisions. If satellites collided, it could create a dangerous amount of space debris, which could cause even more problems for future space missions. SpaceX took these concerns seriously and built systems to help avoid collisions, but the debate over how many satellites should be allowed in orbit continued.

Despite these challenges, Starlink's benefits were clear, especially during difficult times. One major example of this came in 2022 during the Russian invasion of Ukraine. When war broke out, many parts of Ukraine lost access to the Internet, making it hard for people to communicate and for the country's government to stay connected. To help, Elon sent thousands of Starlink terminals — devices that connect to the satellites and provide Internet access — to Ukraine. These terminals helped keep the country online during a time of crisis. In total, about 20,000 terminals were sent to Ukraine, and SpaceX provided the service for free, covering the cost of data transfer, which was around $80 million.

It's amazing to think about how the Internet, something

many of us use every day, can become a lifeline for people in times of need.

However, the cost of continuing to provide Internet service to Ukraine became a concern for SpaceX. In October 2022, Elon asked the U.S. Department of Defense to help cover the costs of sending more Starlink terminals and paying for ongoing service. The request caused some debate, but in the end, Elon publicly stated that SpaceX would continue to provide Starlink to Ukraine for free, even though it would cost the company about $400 million each year.

At the same time, Elon made headlines for another decision related to Starlink during the conflict in Ukraine. While many countries and companies were blocking Russian state media from their platforms due to the war, Elon refused to block Russian media on Starlink. He explained that he believed in free speech and thought that people should be able to access information, even if it came from a government they disagreed with. This decision was controversial, but Elon stood by his belief in the importance of open access to information.

As the war in Ukraine continued, Starlink became even more involved. In September 2023, Ukraine asked Elon to activate Starlink satellites over Crimea, a region that Russia had taken control of, so they could attack Russian naval ships. Elon refused, explaining that he was concerned that such an attack might lead to Russia responding with nuclear weapons. He wanted to avoid escalating the situation to something even more dangerous, so he chose not to allow Starlink to be used in this way.

While Starlink played a key role in global events like the war in Ukraine, its main goal remained the same: to connect people all over the world. Starlink continued to grow, launching more and more satellites into space. By 2023, SpaceX had launched more than 5,000 Starlink satellites, and the service was reaching millions of people across the globe. From remote villages in Africa to far-off islands in the Pacific, Starlink is providing high-speed Internet to places that had never had access before, thus making the world smaller by bringing people together.

Of course, building a global Internet network wasn't easy, and there were still challenges ahead. SpaceX had to keep launching satellites regularly to replace older ones and to expand the network. Each satellite only lasts about five to seven years before it needs to be replaced. This means that the project will need continuous investment to keep it going and growing.

In addition to expanding Starlink's coverage, SpaceX had big plans for improving the service. Elon wanted to make Starlink's Internet speeds even faster and reduce the cost of the terminals so more people could afford them. He also hoped to bring Starlink to airplanes, ships, and other vehicles, so that people could have Internet access even while traveling. Imagine being able to stream a movie or play a game while flying on a plane or sailing across the ocean!

Looking ahead, Starlink's impact on the world could be huge. By connecting people in even the most remote parts of the globe, it could help close the "digital divide," which is the gap between people who have access to the Internet and those who don't. This divide often makes it harder for people in rural or poor areas to get the same opportunities as those in cities, but Starlink could help level the playing field.

By 2023, SpaceX had successfully launched over 5,400 Starlink satellites, though not all of these remained in orbit due to the lifespan of each satellite, which typically lasts between five to seven years. Of those launched, 4,472 are still operational, forming the network that brings global Internet access to millions of people. With around 2.2 million users worldwide, including 1.3 million in the United States, Starlink continues to grow and expand its services, providing Internet to places that have historically struggled to access it.

For Elon Musk, Starlink was another step toward creating a better future. Just like Tesla's electric cars and SolarCity's clean energy, Starlink is all about using technology to solve big problems. Elon believes that the Internet is one of the most powerful tools for education, communication, and innovation, and with Starlink, he is working to make sure everyone can have access to it, no matter where they live.

EIGHT

Neuralink and AI: Blurring the Lines Between Humans and Machines

Always looking forward to a better future, in 2016, Elon Musk turned his attention to something that seemed straight out of a science fiction movie: connecting the human brain with computers and artificial intelligence (AI). Elon is known for thinking big, and he believes that the future of technology could be a lot more powerful if humans and machines could work together in a whole new way. To make this vision a reality, Elon co-founded a company called Neuralink in 2016, when he was forty-five years old. With an investment of $100 million, Elon set Neuralink on a path to explore how advanced technology could interact with the human brain, making it possible for people to do things that once seemed impossible.

So what exactly is Neuralink, and what does it aim to do? Neuralink is a neurotechnology company, which means it focuses on creating technology that can directly connect with the human brain. The idea is to develop devices, called brain-computer interfaces (BCIs), that can be implanted into a person's brain. These devices could help people in many ways, from improving memory to treating brain-related diseases, like Alzheimer's or spinal cord injuries.

Alzheimer's disease is a progressive brain disorder that leads to memory loss, confusion, and difficulty thinking clearly. Over time, it causes the brain to shrink and affects a person's ability to perform daily tasks, communicate, and eventually, even basic functions like swallowing. There is currently no cure for Alzheimer's, but treatments can slow its progression. Neuralink's technology could potentially help by improving memory functions or slowing the degeneration of brain cells.

Spinal cord injuries occur when the spinal cord is damaged, often from accidents or trauma, leading to paralysis or loss of function in parts of the body. This happens because the brain's signals can no longer travel down the spine to control muscles. Neuralink's BCIs could help reconnect these broken pathways, potentially restoring movement and function for people with such injuries by bypassing the damaged spinal cord and allowing the brain to communicate directly with the limbs. Even more futuristic than curing these diseases, Neuralink aims to use these devices to allow humans to communicate with computers and artificial intelligence directly through their thoughts.

Elon's vision for Neuralink goes far beyond just helping people with medical conditions. He believes that in the future, AI could become so advanced that it might surpass human intelligence. This idea has been a concern for Elon, who has warned that if AI gets too powerful, it could be dangerous. So, one of the goals of Neuralink is to ensure that humans can keep up with AI by enhancing their own abilities. By connecting our brains to machines, Elon thinks that humans could work alongside AI instead of being outsmarted by it.

In 2019, Elon announced that Neuralink was working on a device that was similar to a sewing machine but for the brain. This device could carefully place tiny, flexible threads into a person's brain tissue. These threads would be connected to a small chip implanted in the skull, which could send and receive information from the brain. Imagine being able to control a computer, play a video game, or even communicate with others using only your thoughts — this is the incredible vision Neuralink is working toward, and the exciting part is that human trials have already begun! In February 2024, Neuralink made a breakthrough by successfully implanting a brain chip in a human subject. This individual was able to control a computer mouse with his mind, marking a huge step forward in brain-computer interface technology.

This significant progress builds on Neuralink's early developments. By 2020, Neuralink was ready to demonstrate one of its early devices to the public. During a live event, Elon described the device as "a Fitbit in your skull," meaning it was small and could monitor brain activity much like how a Fitbit tracks steps or heart rate. Elon made powerful claims, saying that this technology could soon cure conditions like paralysis, deafness, blindness, and other disabilities.

Many scientists were skeptical of these claims. They pointed out that while the idea of curing such conditions sounded amazing, the technology was still in its early stages, and there was no solid evidence yet that it could deliver on these promises. Some experts called Elon's presentation "neuroscience theater," meaning that it was more of a performance than a real scientific breakthrough. However, Neuralink had shown something impressive: a pig named Gertrude with a Neuralink device implanted in its brain. The device tracked Gertrude's brain activity as she sniffed around, showing that the technology could indeed read signals from a living brain.

In the years that followed, Neuralink continued its research and experiments. One of the most exciting moments came in 2021, when Neuralink released a video showing a monkey, named Pager, playing the video game Pong using only its mind. Pager had a Neuralink device implanted in its brain, and the device allowed the monkey to control the game by thinking about moving the paddle on the screen. This video amazed people around the world and gave a glimpse into what Neuralink might be able to do for humans in the future.

However, while Neuralink's experiments with animals have shown promising results, they've also led to controversy. Some of the monkeys used in the experiments have died, and this raised concerns about how the animals were being treated. The Physicians Committee for Responsible Medicine, a group that advocates for the ethical treatment of animals in medical research, claimed that Neuralink's experiments violated the Animal Welfare Act. They accused the company of causing unnecessary harm to the animals during the experiments. Employees of Neuralink also reported that Elon's desire to speed up the development of the technology had led to mistakes in the experiments, causing more animal deaths than necessary.

Because of these concerns, the U.S. government launched an investigation in 2022 to look into whether Neuralink had broken any animal welfare laws. This investigation put more pressure on Neuralink to ensure that its experiments were safe and ethical, especially as the company prepared for the next big step: testing the technology on humans.

In 2023, Neuralink received approval from the U.S. Food and Drug Administration (FDA) to begin human trials. This was a major milestone for the company, as it would be the first time that their brain-computer interface technology would be tested on people. The trial is expected to last six years, and it will help researchers understand how well the device works in humans and whether it's safe for long-term use. This is an important step toward making the technology available to more people in the future.

Neuralink's work with human trials could eventually lead to breakthroughs in treating some of the most serious medical conditions. For example, people with spinal cord injuries who are unable to move parts of their body could use the device to control robotic limbs or even send signals to their muscles to help them move again. It could also help people with neurological diseases, like Alzheimer's, by improving their memory or communication abilities. In the long run, Neuralink could change the way humans interact with technology and their own bodies.

But as exciting as all of this sounds, there are still many challenges ahead. Developing technology that can safely and effectively interface with the human brain is incredibly difficult. The brain is the most complex organ in the human body, and even small mistakes can lead to serious consequences. There are also ethical concerns about privacy and control. If a device can read someone's thoughts or send signals to their brain, who gets to control that information? What if the device gets hacked? These are questions that will need to be answered as the technology develops.

For Elon, Neuralink is just one part of his larger goal of preparing humanity for the future. He believes that as AI becomes more advanced, humans will need to find new ways to stay competitive and remain in control of their own destiny. By connecting our brains with machines, we could keep pace with AI and maybe even enhance our own abilities. In Elon's view, this technology could help people achieve things that seem impossible today, like curing diseases, boosting brain power, or even merging with AI to become something more than human.

While Neuralink's journey is still in its early stages, it represents a bold step into the unknown. For kids and adults alike, it's exciting to imagine a future where people can use their minds to control technology or overcome physical challenges. The possibilities seem endless, and that's exactly what makes Neuralink so fascinating.

As we look to the future, it's important to think about both the benefits and the risks of technology like Neuralink. What kinds of amazing things could people do if they had the power to control machines with their thoughts? And what challenges might arise as we explore this new frontier? As Neuralink continues to develop, these are the questions that Elon Musk and his team will have to answer, one breakthrough at a time.

NINE

The Hyperloop and Boring Company: Reinventing Transportation

After working on cutting-edge technologies like electric cars, rockets, and BCIs (brain-computer interfaces), Elon Musk turned his attention to a whole new challenge: revolutionizing transportation. While he had already made huge changes with Tesla's electric vehicles, Elon believed that the world needed even more advanced ways to move people quickly and efficiently, especially in crowded cities.

Two of his most innovative ideas in this area were the Hyperloop and The Boring Company, both of which aimed to change the way we think about transportation forever.

The story of Elon's transportation revolution began with the Hyperloop, an idea that sounded almost like something out of a science fiction movie. Elon first introduced the concept of the Hyperloop in 2013. He described it as a high-speed transportation system where people could travel inside pods that zoomed through tubes at incredible speeds. These pods would be placed in low-pressure tubes, which would reduce air resistance and allow them to travel much faster than regular trains. In fact, Elon estimated that the Hyperloop could transport people at speeds of up to 760 miles per hour (about 1,200 kilometers per hour), making it faster than airplanes and much more efficient.

Elon's vision for the Hyperloop was not just about speed; it was also about making transportation cheaper, cleaner, and better for the environment. Unlike traditional trains or planes that run on fuel, the Hyperloop would be powered by renewable energy, like solar power. This would make it a sustainable option for the future, reducing pollution and helping fight climate change. Another big advantage of the Hyperloop was that it could be built above ground on elevated tracks or even underground, which meant it wouldn't take up as much space as regular roads or railways. Elon believed that the Hyperloop could help solve many of the traffic and pollution problems that big cities face today.

But while Elon came up with the idea for the Hyperloop, he didn't have time to develop it himself because he was already so busy running Tesla and SpaceX. So, instead of building the Hyperloop, Elon encouraged other companies and engineers to take his idea and run with it. He made his design plans for the Hyperloop open to the public, allowing anyone who wanted to work on the project to get started. Soon, several companies and student teams around the world began developing their own versions of the Hyperloop, inspired by Elon's original vision.

In the years that followed, companies like Virgin Hyperloop and Hyperloop Transportation Technologies began testing prototypes and working on plans to make the Hyperloop a reality. While there's still a long way to go before people start riding in Hyperloop pods between cities, the idea has captured the imagination of engineers and entrepreneurs all over the world. And who knows — maybe one day, people will be able to travel from city to city at lightning-fast speeds, all thanks to Elon's bold idea.

While the Hyperloop was focused on high-speed travel between cities, Elon also had a vision for improving transportation within cities. This led to the creation of The Boring Company, which Elon founded in 2017. The name might sound funny, but "boring" in this case refers to digging tunnels. Elon's idea was simple: instead of building more roads above ground, why not build a system of tunnels underground where vehicles could travel without getting stuck in traffic?

Traffic jams are a huge problem in many cities around the world. Roads are crowded, and it can take hours to get from one place to another, especially during rush hour. Elon thought that if he could build tunnels deep underground, cars could travel faster without any traffic, and people could get to their destinations much more quickly. His idea was to create a system where cars or special vehicles would enter these tunnels and travel at high speeds, avoiding all the usual traffic problems.

In early 2017, Elon and The Boring Company started discussions with city officials and regulatory bodies to figure out how to build these tunnels. One of the first things they did was dig a test tunnel on the grounds of SpaceX's headquarters. This "test trench" was about thirty feet (9.1 meters) wide, fifty feet (15.2 meters) long, and fifteen feet (4.6 meters) deep, and it gave Elon and his team a chance to practice digging and testing the technology needed to make the tunnels work. Because the trench was built on private property, they didn't need special permits, so they could get started right away.

A little while later, The Boring Company began working on a bigger tunnel in Los Angeles. This tunnel, which was less than two miles long (3.2 kilometers), debuted in 2018 and gave people a first look at what the future of underground transportation might look like. In this demonstration, Tesla cars were used to travel through the tunnel, though they didn't go as fast as originally planned. The ride was also a bit bumpy, which showed that there were still some challenges to overcome before the system could be fully operational.

Even though the initial tests had some issues, Elon didn't give up. He believed that the idea of underground tunnels could still solve many of the problems that cities face with traffic and transportation. Over the next few years, The Boring Company announced plans to build tunnels in several cities, including Chicago and West Los Angeles. Unfortunately, these projects were eventually canceled, mostly due to difficulties with getting permits and approval from local governments.

Despite these setbacks, The Boring Company achieved a major success in Las Vegas. In early 2021, they completed a tunnel beneath the Las Vegas Convention Center, which spans approximately 1.7 miles (2.7 kilometers). This tunnel allowed people to travel across the convention center in Tesla vehicles, avoiding the traffic and crowds above ground. This tunnel was such a success that local officials approved a much larger expansion to create a citywide tunnel system, known as the Vegas Loop. The expanded plan includes about sixty-nine stations covering sixty-five miles (104 kilometers) of tunnels. This project is currently being developed, with stations planned to connect key destinations in Las Vegas such as hotels, casinos, and the airport. When these expansions are completed, people in Las Vegas will be able to travel to different parts of the city quickly and easily by using this underground transportation system.

The Boring Company also explored the idea of creating high-speed tunnels between cities. One idea was to build a tunnel system that could connect Washington, D.C., to New York City. If successful, this could allow people to travel between these two major cities in less than an hour. While this project is still in the planning stages, it shows just how ambitious Elon's vision is for the future of transportation.

At the heart of The Boring Company's mission is the goal of solving one of the biggest problems faced by cities: traffic congestion. By moving vehicles underground and using advanced technology to make the rides faster and smoother, Elon hopes to make travel more efficient and less frustrating for everyone. He believes that this could also reduce pollution and make cities cleaner by cutting down on the number of cars stuck in traffic, spewing exhaust into the air.

One of the exciting aspects of both the Hyperloop and The Boring Company's tunnel system is how they could work together. Imagine a future where you could hop into a high-speed Hyperloop pod to travel between cities and then take an underground tunnel to get across town once you arrive. These two transportation systems could revolutionize how people move, making travel faster, cleaner, and more efficient.

Of course, there are still many challenges to overcome before either the Hyperloop or The Boring Company's tunnels become widely available. Building tunnels is expensive, and it requires approval from governments and local authorities. Additionally, the technology needed to make these systems work perfectly is still being developed.

But if anyone is known for taking on big challenges and pushing the limits of what's possible, it's Elon Musk.

As with many of his other projects, Elon's work with The Boring Company and the Hyperloop is driven by a desire to make the world better for future generations. He envisions a future where people can travel quickly and efficiently without harming the planet. His ideas may seem bold, but they're built on the same principles of innovation and creativity that have helped him succeed in his other ventures.

TEN

Twitter/X: Owning the Biggest Social Media

After working on transforming industries like space travel with SpaceX and transportation with Tesla, Elon Musk turned his attention to something completely different — social media. While Elon had always been active on Twitter, one of the most popular social media platforms, he had long expressed concerns about how it was run.

Elon believed that Twitter was limiting free speech and that it could be a better tool for open communication. Little did anyone know at the time, but Elon would soon go from being a user of Twitter to owning the entire platform.

Elon Musk's interest in buying Twitter wasn't new. As early as 2017, he had mentioned the idea of purchasing the company, believing that it needed changes. But it wasn't until 2022 that Elon made his first serious move toward owning the company.

In January 2022, Elon began quietly buying shares of Twitter. By April of that year, he had bought enough shares to own 9.2 percent of the company, making him the largest shareholder. When this news became public, Twitter's stock price surged, meaning it became more valuable in the stock market. After reaching this milestone, Elon was offered a seat on Twitter's board of directors, meaning he would have some say in how the company was run. As part of the deal, Elon agreed not to buy more than 14.9 percent of Twitter's stock, which would prevent him from taking over the company entirely.

However, just a few days later, Elon changed his mind. Instead of joining the board, he decided he wanted to buy Twitter outright. On April 13, 2022, he made an offer to buy 100 percent of the company for $43 billion, offering $54.20 per share. Elon wanted full control of Twitter so he could make the changes he felt were necessary, including improving free speech and reducing the influence of spam accounts and bots, which are accounts that are not run by real people.

Twitter's board wasn't thrilled with the idea of Elon taking over, so they adopted a strategy called a "poison pill." This plan made it more expensive for any single person to buy more than fifteen percent of the company without the board's approval. But despite this move, Elon continued with his plan, and by the end of April, he had successfully made a deal to buy Twitter for about $44 billion.

To finance this massive purchase, Elon used a combination of loans and his own money. After the deal was announced, things didn't go as smoothly as planned. In May, Elon stated that the deal was "on hold" because he was concerned that Twitter had more fake accounts and spam bots than it had disclosed. Twitter had said that less than five percent of its daily users were spam accounts, but Elon wanted to make sure this was true before finalizing the deal. Although he initially said he was still committed to buying Twitter, by July, he announced that he was terminating the deal altogether.

Twitter's board wasn't happy with this decision, and they decided to sue Elon to force him to follow through with the purchase. The case was filed in the Chancery Court of Delaware, and it looked like there would be a long legal battle ahead. However, in October 2022, just before the case was set to go to trial, Elon changed his mind again and offered to buy Twitter at the original price of $54.20 per share. By the end of October, the deal was finally complete, and Elon officially became the owner of Twitter.

One of Elon's first moves after taking over was to make big changes to Twitter's leadership. He fired several top executives, including the company's CEO, Parag Agrawal, and replaced Agrawal with himself as the new CEO. Elon wanted to take Twitter in a new direction, and he wasted no time getting started.

One of the first major changes Elon made was introducing a new subscription service. For $7.99 a month, users could buy a "blue check" next to their name, which had previously been used to verify the identities of important public figures like celebrities, politicians, and journalists. This change caused some confusion and controversy, as it made it easier for anyone to appear as a verified user. At the same time, Elon's changes to Twitter included significant staff reductions. After acquiring the company, Musk laid off around 80% of Twitter's workforce. This amounted to thousands of employees being let go as part of his efforts to cut costs and restructure the company. Many departments were downsized or eliminated, which led to concerns about the platform's functionality and content moderation capabilities. This large-scale reduction was a crucial part of Musk's overhaul of the social media platform.

Elon also made changes to Twitter's content moderation policies, reducing the level of moderation on the platform. This led to some previously banned accounts becoming unbanned, which sparked a lot of discussion. While some people were happy about the changes, others were concerned that the platform was becoming less safe. Some groups even pointed out that certain harmful or extreme voices were being given more attention, and there were reports that hate speech had increased after Elon took over.

Another major change came in the form of a rebrand. Elon renamed the platform "X" as part of his vision to transform Twitter into more than just a social media platform. He wanted "X" to become a place where people could do everything from communicating to shopping to banking, all within one app. The name change marked a new chapter in Twitter's history, but it also came with its own set of challenges.

By the end of 2022, Elon was facing increased pressure as CEO of Twitter. In December, he posted a poll on Twitter asking users whether he should step down as CEO, promising to follow their decision. The majority of users voted that he should step down, and in May 2023, he did just that. Elon appointed Linda Yaccarino, a former executive at NBC Universal (National Broadcasting Company Universal), as the new CEO of Twitter, while Elon shifted his role to executive chairman and chief technology officer.

Running Twitter, or "X" as it's now called, wasn't without its difficulties. The company faced financial struggles, especially because Elon had borrowed $13 billion to finance the purchase. In August 2024, the Wall Street Journal reported that this deal was now considered one of the worst in merger finance history. Elon's bold move to buy Twitter hadn't gone according to plan, and by September 2024, it was reported that Twitter had lost $24 billion in value, a huge drop from what the company was once worth.

Despite the setbacks, Elon remains committed to his vision for X. While the road ahead for the platform is filled with challenges, Elon sees X as an opportunity to create something entirely new in the world of social media. He believes that by combining his ideas for free speech, technology, and innovation, X can eventually become a platform unlike anything else.

ELEVEN

The Man Behind the Mask

Elon Musk might seem like a superhero, juggling companies and revolutionizing transportation and mankind itself. But behind all the big ideas, bold moves, and futuristic technology, Elon Musk is also a human being, with a life full of ups and downs just like anyone else. From his family to his personal relationships, his story shows that even the most successful people face challenges and difficult decisions.

Elon Musk has had a large family, with at least twelve children. His first wife, Canadian author Justine Wilson, was a big part of his early family life. However, after eight years of marriage, they divorced in 2008. During their marriage, they had six sons. Their first child, Nevada, tragically passed away as an infant, and later they had twins Griffin and Xavier in 2004, followed by triplets Kai, Saxon, and Damian in 2006. Despite their separation, they continued to share custody of their children and co-parented amicably.

After his divorce from Justine, Elon's personal life continued to make headlines. In 2008, he began dating English actress Talulah Riley. Their relationship was an interesting one, full of ups and downs. They married in 2010 in a beautiful ceremony in Scotland, but just two years later, they divorced. Surprisingly, they rekindled their relationship and remarried in 2013, only to divorce again in 2016. Despite the on-and-off nature of their relationship, Elon and Talulah remained close for many years, even though they did not have any children together.

In 2017, Elon briefly dated actress Amber Heard, though their relationship was short-lived. Around this time, Elon's personal life began to attract more media attention, not just because of who he was dating but also because of the massive changes happening in his career. Tesla was growing, SpaceX was reaching new heights, and Elon was quickly becoming one of the most talked-about figures in the tech world!

In 2018, Elon began dating Canadian musician Grimes, whose real name is Claire Boucher. Their relationship made waves, especially because Grimes is known for her unique style and creative music. In 2020, they had a son, whose name quickly became a topic of conversation. They named him "X Æ A-12," a combination of letters and numbers that represented different meanings, including references to technology and space. The unusual name didn't quite follow the rules for naming a child in California, so they changed it slightly to "X Æ A-Xii," which is pronounced as "X Ash A Twelve." Despite the name change, the couple received some criticism for choosing such a complex name for their child.

This eccentric choice of name, though surprising to many, perfectly captures Elon's vision of the future and his desire to break away from traditional norms. Just as Elon pushes the boundaries of technology and space exploration, his personal life reflects a forward-thinking mindset that's focused on innovation and the unknown. Choosing such a futuristic name for his child hints at his belief that the next generation will live in a world vastly different from todays — a world shaped by technology, exploration, and possibilities that seem limitless. It's a glimpse into the mind of a person who not only wants to take the world forward but also sees the future as something worth embracing in every aspect of life.

Moreover, some celebrities choose unique or eccentric names for their children to maintain privacy and reduce media attention. Unconventional names can make it harder for the public or paparazzi to easily identify their children. For Elon Musk and Grimes, naming their child "X Æ A-12" not only reflects their futuristic, tech-focused worldview, but also adds a layer of anonymity. By avoiding a traditional name, they may be trying to shield their child from public scrutiny, echoing a broader trend among public figures who prioritize privacy for their child.

Elon and Grimes continued their relationship, and in 2021, they had a second child, a daughter. However, by the time their daughter, Exa Dark Sideræl Musk, was born, Elon and Grimes had already described their relationship as "semi-separated." In interviews, they explained that their relationship was fluid, meaning it didn't follow the typical rules of dating or marriage. Their relationship remained in the public eye, and in 2023, it was reported that they had a third child together, a son named Tau Techno Mechanicus Musk.

Elon's family continued to grow in unexpected ways. In 2022, news broke that Elon had twins with Shivon Zilis, an executive at Neuralink, the company Elon co-founded to explore brain-computer interfaces. Elon embraced his growing family and welcomed these new additions. The twins were named Strider and Azure, adding to Elon's ever-expanding family.

Elon's relationships with his birth family have also been complex. He has spoken about becoming estranged from his father, Errol Musk, after years of difficulties, though specifics have remained largely private. However, Elon's mother, Maye Musk, a well-known model and nutritionist, continues to be a strong and positive presence in his life. Elon has also mentioned having a supportive relationship with his siblings, particularly his brother Kimbal Musk, with whom he shares a close bond. Kimbal has been involved in various business ventures alongside Elon, while their sister Tosca Musk has built a career in filmmaking. Despite busy lives, Elon maintains connections with his family members while juggling his personal and professional commitments.

Elon's personal life, with its many relationships and large family, might seem complicated to some, but it reflects the challenges and choices that many people face when balancing family and career. Elon is a busy man, running multiple companies and constantly working on new projects, but he has spoken about his love for his children and his desire to give them the best opportunities in life.

Beyond his family life, Elon Musk has also become a well-known public figure. While many billionaires prefer to stay out of the spotlight, Elon often shares his thoughts, ideas, and even jokes on social media, especially on X. His online presence has made him a polarizing figure — some people admire his boldness and honesty, while others find his comments controversial. Elon isn't afraid to make statements that stir up debate, and he's often described as a mix of philosopher and "troll" on social media.

Elon's influence on popular culture is undeniable. In fact, his personality and accomplishments even inspired the character Tony Stark, also known as Iron Man, in the *Marvel* movies. The character of Tony Stark, portrayed by Robert Downey Jr., is a brilliant inventor and entrepreneur who uses his technology to save the world. Elon himself made a cameo appearance in the 2010 movie *Iron Man 2*, and many fans have compared the real-life Elon to the fictional Tony Stark.

Elon's fame has led to other appearances in movies and TV shows as well. He's made cameos in movies like *Machete Kills* and *Men in Black: International*, and he's appeared on TV shows like *The Simpsons, The Big Bang Theory,* and *Rick and Morty*. In 2021, he even hosted *Saturday Night Live*, showing off his sense of humor and playful side to a wide audience.

But while Elon enjoys the spotlight, he's also received many awards and honors for his contributions to science and technology. He's been recognized by organizations like the American Institute of Aeronautics and Astronautics, the Royal Aeronautical Society, and the National Academy of Engineering. In 2021, *Time* magazine named him "Person of the Year," celebrating his influence on both life on Earth and potentially life beyond Earth. Elon's work with Tesla, SpaceX, and other ventures has changed industries and opened up new possibilities for the future.

Even though Elon has achieved incredible things, he's still a regular person with hobbies and interests. He enjoys playing video games, and some of his favorites include *Quake, Diablo IV,* and *Elden Ring*. Like many people, he uses games as a way to relax and unwind, showing that even the busiest people need time to have fun.

Elon's life isn't without its challenges, though. He has openly spoken about his struggles with occasional depression, and there have been reports that he uses medications to manage his mental health. Elon has said that he wants to be honest about these challenges because they're a part of his life, and he believes it's important to acknowledge them.

Through it all, Elon Musk remains a fascinating figure. He's a man who has changed the world in many ways, from electric cars to space exploration, and he's not afraid to take risks or dream big. But behind the mask of success and fame, he's also a father, a thinker, and a person who faces the same kinds of struggles as anyone else. His story shows that even those who seem larger than life have their own personal journeys filled with triumphs and setbacks.

In the end, Elon Musk's life is a reminder that great achievements don't come without challenges, and that being human means experiencing the full range of emotions — joy, sadness, success, and failure. As he continues to push the boundaries of what's possible, both on Earth and beyond, Elon Musk remains a figure who inspires, challenges, and sparks curiosity in people all over the world.

Conclusion

Elon Musk's journey from a young boy with big dreams in South Africa to one of the most influential figures in the world is nothing short of remarkable. He has reshaped industries, pushed the boundaries of what we believe is possible, and inspired countless people to dream bigger. Through his work with companies like SpaceX, Tesla, Neuralink, and The Boring Company, Elon has shown that the future is something we can create if we are bold enough to take risks and work hard.

From rockets that can be reused to electric cars that are revolutionizing the way we travel, Elon has always had his sights set on solving humanity's greatest challenges. His vision for the future includes a world powered by clean energy, people living on multiple planets, and technology that helps humans overcome both physical and mental barriers. But even as he focuses on these massive goals, Elon is always looking for ways to improve everyday life — whether it's by making transportation faster and easier, connecting the world through the Internet, or giving people the tools to harness the power of their own minds.

What makes Elon Musk truly special isn't just his success, but his willingness to keep pushing forward, even when faced with setbacks or failure. His story is full of challenges — from financial struggles to personal setbacks — and yet, he never gives up. He learns from his mistakes, adapts, and continues moving toward his goal of making the future brighter for everyone.

For smart kids like you, Elon Musk's story shows that there's no limit to what you can achieve if you follow your curiosity and never stop asking big questions. Whether you want to build the next great invention, explore new worlds, or make the Earth a better place to live, the possibilities are endless. Elon's life reminds us that it's okay to think differently, to take risks, and to dream of things that others might think are impossible.

As you go forward on your own journey, remember that the future is being shaped right now, and you can be a part of it. Just like Elon Musk, you have the power to change the world with your ideas, your passion, and your dedication. The next big breakthrough could come from you, and who knows — you might even help take humanity to Mars and beyond.

Fun Facts About Elon Musk

1. Almost Sold Tesla to Google

In 2013, when Tesla was struggling, Elon Musk nearly sold the company to Google for $6 billion. Fortunately, the deal never happened, and Tesla went on to become a major success.

2. He Dropped Out of Stanford

Elon Musk attended Stanford University for just two days before deciding to drop out. He was initially pursuing a PhD in Physics but left to start his first company, Zip2, which he sold four years later for more than $300 million.

3. He Owns a James Bond Car

In 2013, Musk bought a Lotus Esprit from the James Bond movie *The Spy Who Loved Me* for almost $1 million. It's the car that turns into a submarine in the film, and Musk has admitted it helped inspire the design of Tesla's Cybertruck.

4. He Named His Son After Professor Xavier

One of Musk's sons, Xavier, was named after Professor Xavier from the *X-Men* comics, showing his love for superheroes and sci-fi.

5. He Has Asperger's Syndrome

Elon Musk revealed that he has Asperger's syndrome, a form of autism, a form of autism that affects how people communicate and interact with others. He mentioned that it shaped how he grew up and sometimes made social interactions more challenging for him.

6. He Doesn't Take a Salary

As CEO of Tesla, Musk doesn't take a traditional salary. Instead, his wealth is based on Tesla stock and the growth of his companies.

7. His Tesla Is Floating in Space

In 2018, Musk launched his personal Tesla Roadster into space on a Falcon Heavy rocket. The car is still out there, orbiting the Sun, with a mannequin named "Starman" in the driver's seat.

8. He Has Over 140,000 People Working for Him

As of 2023, Elon Musk's companies employ tens of thousands of people globally. For example:

- Tesla has around 127,855 employees.
- SpaceX employs approximately 12,000 people.
- Neuralink has a smaller team, with a few hundred employees.
- The Boring Company and other ventures also employ several hundred people.

In total, it's estimated that over 140,000 people work across all of Musk's ventures, contributing to his ambitious projects in space, transportation, energy, and more.

9. He Has Been the Richest Man in the World

Thanks to his work with Tesla, SpaceX, and other ventures, Elon Musk has frequently held the title of the richest person on Earth. His fortune has soared to over $180 billion at times!

Timeline of Elon Musk's Life

June 28, 1971: Elon Musk is born in Pretoria, South Africa.

1980: Elon's parents divorce, and Elon decides to live with his father, Errol Musk.

1981: Elon gets his first computer, a Commodore VIC-20, and teaches himself programming.

1984: At the age of twelve, Elon creates and sells his first video game, *Blastar*, for $500.

1989: At seventeen, Elon moves to Canada to attend Queen's University in Ontario, leaving behind South Africa.

1992: Transfers to the University of Pennsylvania, where he earns degrees in Physics and Economics.

1995: Elon moves to Silicon Valley, attends Stanford University for two days, then drops out to start his first company, Zip2.

1999: Zip2 is sold for $307 million, earning Elon $22 million. He co-founds X.com, which later becomes PayPal.

2002: PayPal is sold to eBay for $1.5 billion. Elon earns $175 million from the sale. He uses $100 million to start SpaceX.

2004: Elon invests $6.35 million in Tesla Motors, becoming its largest shareholder and later its chairman.

2006: Helps create SolarCity, a solar energy services company, founded by his cousins with Elon's backing.

2008: SpaceX successfully launches its first rocket into space after three failed attempts. Elon becomes Tesla's CEO.

2010: Tesla goes public, raising $226 million in its IPO (Initial Public Offering).

2012: Tesla releases the Model S, which becomes a critical and commercial success.

2015: SpaceX successfully lands the first reusable rocket, changing the future of space travel.

2016: Elon co-founds Neuralink, a company focused on connecting the human brain with computers. Tesla acquires SolarCity.

2017: Elon starts The Boring Company to create underground transportation systems and reduce traffic congestion.

2018: SpaceX launches the Falcon Heavy rocket with Elon's Tesla Roadster onboard, sending it into space.

2019: Neuralink unveils its brain-machine interface technology, demonstrating progress with animal trials.

2020: SpaceX becomes the first private company to send astronauts to the International Space Station with its crew Dragon spacecraft.

2020: Starlink, SpaceX's satellite Internet project, starts providing Internet to rural areas.

2022: Elon completes the acquisition of Twitter for $44 billion dollars and becomes CEO of the platform (later rebranded to X).

2023: Tesla begins delivering the first Cybertrucks to customers, a long-awaited addition to its vehicle lineup.

References

Biography Editors. *Elon Musk*. Biography (2022). https://www.
biography.com/business-leaders/elon-musk. Accessed October 4th,
2024.

Cohen, Jenny and Kissell, Chris. *20 Surprising Facts About Elon Musk*.
Finance Buzz (2024). https://financebuzz.com/elon-musk-facts.
Accessed October 8th, 2024.

Easto, Jessica. *Rocket Man: Elon Musk In His Own Words (In Their Own
Words)*. New York. Agate Publishing, 2017.

Gregersen, Erik. *Elon Musk*. Britannica (2024). https://www.britannica.
com/money/Elon-Musk. Accessed October 10th, 2024.

Isaacson, Walter. *Elon Musk*. New York. Simon & Schuster, 2023.

Kumar, Abhishek. *Elon Musk: A Complete Biography*. PRABHAT
PRAKASHAN PVT Limited, 2022.

Vlismas, Michael. *Elon Musk: Risking it All*. London. Jonathan Ball
Publishers, 2022.

Wikipedia contributors. *Elon Musk*. Wikipedia (2024). https://en.
wikipedia.org/wiki/Elon_Musk. Accessed October 5th, 2024.

BONUS

Check out my other book, *Leonardo da Vinci: A Book for Smart Kids*, and learn about the inspiring life of one of history's greatest leaders. As a bonus, you get the introduction and first chapter right here. Enjoy!

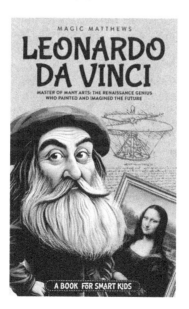

INTRODUCTION

Have you ever wondered what it would be like to be a genius who could paint incredible masterpieces, design futuristic machines, and discover the secrets of nature? That's exactly what Leonardo da Vinci did more than 500 years ago! He wasn't just a painter; he was a scientist, engineer, inventor, and thinker who explored every corner of his imagination.

In *Leonardo da Vinci: A Book For Smart Kids - Master of Many Arts: The Renaissance Genius Who Painted and Imagined the Future*, you'll get to know Leonardo da Vinci, the man who lived during the exciting time of the Renaissance (1450-1600), a period when people were rediscovering art, science, and new ways of thinking. You'll travel through his life, from his early days as a curious boy in Italy to becoming one of the most famous artists and inventors the world has ever known. Along the way, you'll learn about his incredible paintings, like the *Mona Lisa* and *The Last Supper*, and the brilliant ideas he sketched out in his notebooks, many of which wouldn't become reality until hundreds of years later!

But what made Leonardo so special wasn't just his amazing talents — it was his endless curiosity and imagination. He wanted to know how everything worked, from the way birds flew to how the human body moved. His mind never stopped wondering, and that's why his legacy still shines so brightly today.

This book will take you on an adventure through Leonardo's life, showing how one person's creativity and desire to learn can change the world. Are you ready to be inspired by a genius? Let's dive into the incredible story of Leonardo da Vinci!

Leonardo da Vinci was born on April 15, 1452, in a small village called Vinci, about twenty miles (approximately thirty-two kilometers) from Florence, Italy. This was more than 570 years ago, during a time known as the Renaissance — a period of great change and discovery in Europe, especially in art, science, and learning. Religion, too, played a central role in daily life, as the Catholic Church wielded immense power and influence over both spiritual and political matters, shaping the intellectual and cultural landscape of the era. Leonardo's full name was Leonardo di ser Piero da Vinci, which means "Leonardo, son of Piero from Vinci." He wasn't born into a wealthy or famous family; in fact, he was born out of wedlock. This means that Leonardo's parents were not married when he was born, which was uncommon back then. Being born out of wedlock could sometimes affect a child's opportunities, but Leonardo's father still made sure he was taken care of.

Leonardo's father, Piero da Vinci, was a well-respected legal notary in Florence. A legal notary is someone who helps make important documents official, such as contracts, agreements, or wills. In those days, notaries wrote and kept records of these documents, making sure they were fair and followed the law. Piero was highly respected for this work, which was very important in helping people with legal issues. Leonardo's mother, Caterina, came from a lower-class family, and although little is known about her, it's believed that she later married a local man and was only minutely involved in Leonardo's life. Shortly after his birth, Leonardo's parents married other people, and Leonardo went to live with his father's origin family, including his grandfather and uncles.

Leonardo grew up in the charming village of Vinci, located in the heart of Tuscany, Italy. Vinci was a typical small, rural village, known for its peaceful surroundings and picturesque landscapes. The village was nestled among rolling hills covered with vineyards, olive groves, and cypress trees, creating a tranquil and inspiring environment. The region's warm climate made it perfect for farming, and many people in Vinci lived simple, agricultural lives.

Vinci was also home to small stone houses, winding pathways, and medieval towers, giving it a timeless, almost storybook-like quality. The rural setting, with its slow-paced life and connection to nature, offered young Leonardo endless opportunities to explore. He spent his early years wandering through the fields, observing how water flowed through streams, watching birds in flight, and studying the intricate details of plants and animals around him. This quiet, natural setting nurtured his deep curiosity and love for the world, which later became the foundation for both his artistic and scientific achievements.

When Leonardo was still very young, he spent a little time living with his mother, Caterina, and her husband, Antonio di Piero Buti del Vacca, in a nearby village. However, by the time he was around five years old, he started living permanently in the household of his paternal grandfather, Antonio da Vinci. Living with his grandfather meant that Leonardo was surrounded by his father's family, but his father, Piero, wasn't around often. Piero spent most of his time in Florence, where he had a successful career as a notary. Although Leonardo didn't see his father often, his uncle, Francesco da Vinci, played an important role in his early life. Francesco was much closer in age to Leonardo — being about sixteen years older — and the two had a strong bond.

When Leonardo was still a child, his father, Piero, remarried several times, and as a result, Leonardo had many half-brothers and sisters. Piero eventually had at least twelve children with his wives, making Leonardo the eldest of a large, blended family. However, despite having many siblings, Leonardo didn't grow up close to them. His father's focus was on his legal career in Florence, and Leonardo was primarily raised by his grandfather and uncle in Vinci, while his half-siblings were born later into Piero's other families.

Leonardo's relationship with his half-brothers became more significant later in his life. After their father died in 1504, Leonardo was involved in a dispute with his half-brothers over their father's estate, creating some tension among them. This separation and difference in upbringing meant that Leonardo's strongest family connection during his early years was not with his half-siblings but with his uncle, Francesco, who shared his love for nature and the outdoors and nurtured Leonardo's growing curiosity.

From an early age, Leonardo showed a deep curiosity about everything around him. He was fascinated by the natural world — plants, animals, water, and even the sky. He would spend hours observing the way birds flew or the way water moved through streams. This love for learning and observation stayed with him his entire life and influenced much of his later work.

Unlike many children of wealthy families, Leonardo didn't receive a formal education. At that time, boys from wealthy or noble families typically attended schools where they studied subjects like Latin, philosophy, and advanced mathematics. School was often focused on preparing students for careers in law, politics, or the church. Lessons were strict, with students spending long hours memorizing texts, reciting lessons, and practicing their writing skills with quills. Latin was the language of scholars, so learning it was crucial for those who wanted to work in prestigious fields. However, Leonardo's education was more informal. He learned to read and write in the local language, Italian, instead of Latin, and he studied basic mathematics. Most importantly, his real education came from his keen observations of the world around him, where he developed the skills that would set him apart as an artist and an inventor. His artistic talent became obvious at a young age, and his family recognized that he had a special gift. They decided to focus on nurturing his artistic abilities rather than giving him the standard education.

One of the earliest memories Leonardo recorded later in life was of a kite, a type of bird, flying down and brushing its tail across his face when he was just a baby in his cradle. This story might sound a bit fantastical, and some people debate whether it was a real memory or something Leonardo imagined. But whether real or not, it shows how deeply Leonardo felt connected to the natural world from the beginning.

As Leonardo grew older, his interest in nature and the world only deepened. He spent countless hours exploring the countryside around Vinci, collecting plants, drawing animals, and studying how things worked. He didn't just look at things — he wanted to understand them. Why did birds fly the way they did? How did water flow and create patterns? These kinds of questions filled Leonardo's mind and inspired him to experiment and investigate.

While living with his grandfather and uncle, Leonardo didn't have the distractions of a busy city, which gave him plenty of time to observe and learn. From a young age, he began to sketch and draw. At first, his drawings were simple, but even at a young age, his incredible attention to detail set him apart from other children. He didn't just draw what he saw; he captured the beauty and complexity of the world with remarkable precision.

Living in the countryside also gave Leonardo a close connection to nature, which became a central theme in his work later on. He was always looking for patterns in the world — whether it was the spiral of a shell or the veins of a leaf. These observations helped him become a great artist, an inventor, and a scientist.

Leonardo's curiosity wasn't limited to nature, though. He was also fascinated by people — how they moved, how their bodies worked, and how their emotions showed on their faces. From a young age, he started drawing people, paying close attention to their expressions and gestures.

This skill became incredibly important when he started painting, as he was able to bring his subjects to life in a way that few other artists could.

Even though Leonardo didn't have a formal education, his learning never stopped. He was a boy who loved to ask questions and figure out how things worked. He didn't just accept the world as it was; he wanted to understand it on a deeper level. And this desire to learn and explore made him stand out from others.

Leonardo's father, Piero, eventually recognized that his son had a remarkable talent for art. In those days, becoming an artist was a highly respected and important profession. Artists were not just painters; they were creators who designed buildings, sculptures, and even military equipment. Their skills were in high demand by wealthy patrons, churches, and governments, who commissioned them to create beautiful works of art that would last for centuries. To become a successful artist, however, required years of training under a master to learn the techniques of drawing, painting, and sculpting. This extensive training prepared artists to make a living through their work and contribute to society in many ways. So, when Leonardo was around fourteen years old, his father arranged for him to become an apprentice in the workshop of Andrea del Verrocchio, one of the most famous artists in Florence at the time. This was a huge opportunity for Leonardo, and it marked the beginning of his journey as an artist and inventor.

Thanks for being a reader!

If you enjoyed reading *Elon Musk: A Book For Smart Kids*, I'd love to hear what you think! Leaving a review on Amazon is like giving the book a high-five — and it helps other readers find it too. Plus, it's super quick! Just scan the QR code to get started.

Thanks for being awesome and sharing your thoughts!

Magic Matthews

Made in the USA
Monee, IL
14 January 2025

76787273R00075